CW01643207

ECHO OF SOULS

London
2024

Book Title:

Followed by official details of the book. Pages to run back to back

To Zaga.

Your support is Greatly appreciated.

Enjoy!

[illegible]

10/10/24

Dedication

This book is dedicated to my daughters Tolulope, Oluwatosin and Mosebolatan Beckley.

Acknowledgement

I wish to express my sincere appreciation to Liz and Terry Boley for their consistent warmth, wisdom, and support in guiding me through the fulfilling journey of becoming an author. Their encouragement has been invaluable to me.

I am also profoundly thankful for the enduring friendship and support of Wendy and Debbie Clarke-Whyatt, Marc Jackson, Sandra Hibbert, and Stacey Shelley. Their belief in me and my work has been a source of great strength. I would also like to thank Funmi Beckley for generously contributing her time and expertise to the book's typesetting.

Lastly, I am deeply grateful to my family and friends for their instrumental roles in this new chapter of my life. Their unwavering support has meant the world to me and has driven my pursuit of this new career.

Foreword

Theo had a tumultuous start to his life. He was left orphaned and alone in the world at a tender age and had to fend for himself in the harsh streets. Life had dealt him a cruel hand, and he was forced to grow up faster than most young people his age. Despite the overwhelming odds, Theo did not give up on his dreams of a better life.

One of Theo's biggest obstacles was the lack of formal education. He was denied the opportunity to attend school without any parents to support him. It was a bitter pill, but he refused to let it get the better of him. Instead, he resolved to educate himself by any means necessary. During this time, he met a retired school teacher who would change the course of his life. The good Samaritan noticed Theo's thirst for knowledge and offered to give him voluntary weekly tuition. Theo was grateful for the teaching support and displayed a keenness for learning that impressed his teacher.

Despite his challenges, Theo persevered and built a foundation of knowledge that would serve him well in the years to come. His teacher's kindness had given him a glimmer of hope and a sense of purpose that he had never felt before. It was a turning point in his young life that he would always be grateful for.

Table of Content

Chapter 1

Abandonment

A constant struggle marked Theo's childhood for survival, as he was born into a small remote village offering little support. From the moment he took his first breath, he was left to fend for himself, with no parents to provide the love and care that every child deserves. Theo remained resilient and determined to improve his situation despite the harsh conditions. But the absence of a family left a gaping hole in his life that he could never fill. He often longed for the warmth of a parental embrace, the comfort of a home-cooked meal, or the companionship of siblings. Yet, these things remained out of his reach as he was left to navigate the world alone. Theo was a small, unnourished, and fragile-looking boy, with his ribs protruding from his body. He had no access to education, no adult to watch over him, no food to fill his stomach, and no one to turn to for help, except for one true friend who never left his side. Despite his challenging circumstances, Theo tried his best to survive alone. But when he turned twelve years old, a miraculous event occurred that would alter the course of his life forever.

It was a cold winter morning in December, and Theo was sitting on the pavement with his head buried in a book when his best friend Vaney appeared. Vaney, a grown adult once a teacher, lost her job and now spends her time helping less fortunate people like Theo. Whenever she passed by him, she would offer him food and money or teach him something new. Theo looked forward to her visits, three times a week, when she would personally teach him things he had never learned. He was a curious boy, eager to soak up knowledge, and to him, Vaney felt like the closest thing he had to a family.

One day, however, Vaney arrived with a look of anxiety on her face. Theo noticed that she did not have her usual stack of books with her. Instead, she told Theo that a terrible rainstorm was coming, which could potentially flood the entire town in the next three days. The streets were chaotic, with people rushing to stock up on supplies and prepare to evacuate. Theo felt a surge of fear as he realised he had nowhere to go. Vaney could sense his fear and quickly came up with a solution. She invited him to stay with her and her family until the storm passed. Theo was ecstatic at the idea of having a roof over his head for the first time. He eagerly agreed, and they both walked back to Vaney's house together, leaving the cold streets behind.

As they walked, Theo couldn't help but feel grateful for Vaney. She had always been there for him, offering him kindness and knowledge when no one else would. Now, she was giving him a place to stay during a difficult time, proving once again that she was the closest thing he had to a family.

"I live in this apartment; sorry if you expected a two-story building," Vaney said, sighing. "Oh, don't be sorry. I love it. I'm just glad to have a roof over my head," Theo replied, trying to make her feel better. He slowly walked into the flat, attempting to show enthusiasm, but had a wrong first impression. Toys littered the floor, making it challenging to move around. Six people were crammed into the tiny space, as it seemed they might have been better off sleeping on the streets. "Theo, these are my two sons: Roger, who's nine, and Kayode, who's seven," Vaney introduced them. "Hello, Kayode and Roger," Theo said politely, but the boys didn't reply and returned to playing with their toys. "And this is my mother and father, but you can call them Mama and Pappi," Vaney said. "Hello, Mama and Pappi," Theo said.

"My goodness! You are as skinny as a stick. I could eat you whole. Vaney, we need to put some meat on those bones!" Vaney's mother implied. Theo smiled while Vaney's mother returned to her knitting, and her father kept his eyes on the television. The sofas Vaney's parents sat on were low to the ground, and rips were everywhere. A thick layer of dust covered every surface, and the cramped kitchen was dirty, with dirty dishes piling up in and out of the sink. Cereal boxes were left out, and there were crumbs on the table.

As Vaney offered Theo some food, he couldn't help but explore the house. After all, he was curious about where she lived with her family. Theo felt hungry, so he requested a sandwich, and Vaney kindly agreed to make one for him. While she prepared the meal, Theo wandered around the house and stumbled upon a bedroom. As he entered, he noticed that it was pretty cramped. The room had two double beds, probably for Vaney and her parents, and two single beds for her children. The closet was small, and it seemed like they had to cram all their clothes. Theo then moved to the bathroom, and the sight that greeted him was pretty unpleasant. The damp towels were lying on the bathroom floor alongside bits of toilet paper and toothbrushes. The shower drain had hairs around it, and some toothpaste was still left in the sink. Theo felt disgusted as he realised that Vaney had been living in such awful conditions.

Vaney then asked Theo his opinion of her place; he didn't want to hurt her feelings, so he lied and complimented the place. Theo sat on the sofa to eat his sandwich as the table was quite messy. Mama enjoyed her peanut butter and jelly sandwich and asked Theo if he liked it. After finishing his meal, Theo tried to converse with Kayode and Roger, who were also in the house.

Theo looked over at Kayode and Roger, who was deeply engrossed in building a Lego dinosaur. "What are you playing?" he asked, curious. Roger looked up and replied, "We are making our Lego dinosaur that we got from Mama and Papa." Theo's eyes lit up with excitement as he asked, "May I help?" The two brothers exchanged a hesitant look before glancing over at their mum, who gave them a stern look that made it clear they had no choice but to let Theo join them. They sighed and said, "Okay, but you can't touch anything unless we tell you to. Understood?" Kayode then warned, "We will be right back. Don't touch anything!"

As the boys walked away, Vaney yelled, "Come and take your vitamins!" Theo couldn't resist the urge to join in, so he tried to place some pieces that looked like they would fit. However, as he did, some tiny pieces went under the sofa as Pappi walked past him. Theo turned to look, but it was too late; he accidentally knocked over the dinosaur, and it broke into pieces. When the boys returned, they were both angry and upset. "We were only gone for two seconds, and you ruined our time-consuming model! Where are half of the pieces?" Roger shouted.

Theo pointed under the sofa, but it was too late; half of the pieces were already lost. Roger was about to burst out in anger when Theo apologised and offered to buy them a new one. However, Theo blamed Pappi for walking past and pushing some pieces under the sofa. At that moment, Vaney walked in, relieved Theo, and asked, "What's going on here?"

Roger accused Theo of breaking their toy and losing some of its pieces. Vaney, the mother, tried to calm the boys down, telling them that it was likely an accident and that Theo would never do something like that on purpose. However, Roger insisted that Theo was responsible for the damage. Vaney became frustrated and scolded the boys, instructing them to go to bed. Theo felt guilty and confessed the truth to Vaney, explaining that he didn't want to be seen as a troublemaker and get kicked out. Vaney reassured Theo that she wouldn't kick him out and forgave him for the accident.

Despite this, the boys still felt guilty and wanted to clear the air. Roger explained that Theo didn't intentionally break the toy but accidentally knocked it over while trying to retrieve some of the lost pieces hidden under the sofa. The boys' grandfather, pappi, had also knocked some of the pieces under the couch, contributing to the accident. Vaney was grateful for the honesty and punished the boys by sending them to bed until tea time. Despite feeling bad for the boys, Theo was glad they had told the truth and resolved the situation.

"Theo, you have two entertainment options- you can watch TV or read one of Roger's childhood books. These books were treasured by Roger when he was only five years old. Unlike Roger, Roger used to read a lot. He is more disciplined and sensible, although he sometimes gets cranky. These books are easy to read, and based on everything I have taught you, I'm confident you'll be able to read them easily," Vaney explained gently. Theo replied with a nod of his head, indicating his understanding. Vaney observed Theo's facial expressions and realised that he was feeling a bit anxious. She decided to ease his nerves by assuring him he could enjoy the books without any pressure.

After about twenty minutes, Vaney relieved the boys of their punishment. The boys were delighted and started to search for the scattered pieces of their Lego dinosaur. Suddenly, the room's aura changed with the arrival of a man dressed in a white shirt with black trousers, a navy blue and white striped tie, and a big black briefcase. The man's severe expression made Vaney and the boys feel apprehensive. “Hello, Vaney, Roger, and Kayode,” the man said in a deep voice.

“Hi, Patrick. Theo, this is my husband, Patrick. Patrick, this is Theo, the homeless boy I go to tutor three times a week,’ Vaney introduced Theo. “Daddy!” the boys shouted, excitedly running up to Patrick and hugging him.

“Hello, Theo. Are you living with us now?” he assumed, pulling the boys off him. “Now, Patrick, don’t be rude to our guest. Theo will stay with us until we can return to the city after the rain storm,’ Vaney said. “But we don’t have space in our car,” Patrick complained. “Let’s not worry about the future. For now, let us all relax and get to know Theo”, Vaney insisted, “I’ll get a start on dinner. We’re having spaghetti and tomato sauce. Is that all right, Theo?” “That’s lovely. I have never had a home-cooked meal before. I’m sure it will be lovely”, he said nicely. “Theo, while Vaney makes dinner, do you want a warm shower and clean yourself up?” Patrick interrogated.

"Sure", he answered. Theo walked to the bathroom without questions and had his first shower, which he loved…

"Everyone, come and eat!" Vaney cried out. Mama, Pappi, Patrick, Roger, and Theo rushed to the table within seconds. There were only four seats at the table, so after everyone poured in their food, Mama, pappi, and Patrick sat on the small, ripped sofa while the rest sat on the table. Quietly, everyone ate their delicious-looking food, and the only noise you could hear was the TV. Mama and Pappi watched an old show without colour, professional lighting, or studio. It was an ancient film. Not long after they all finished eating, Vaney broke the silence. "Did you enjoy your food, Theo?" she asked. Theo replied, "Yes, I did. It was very nice. Thank you." "You're very welcome,' she said. "Uh, Vaney, where will I sleep?" Theo queried. "Oh…uh, you can sleep with me in a double bed if you want",' Vaney said. "But then where will I sleep?" Patrick butted in. Vaney said serenely, "You can sleep on the couch until we get a sleeping bag or an air mattress." "We don't have space for an air mattress," Patrick growled. "So then you will have to sleep on a sleeping bag. We can get one tomorrow", Vaney's father intruded randomly. Patrick was slightly irritated and decided it was best not to argue back.

It had been two hours since dinner, and during that time, Roger and Kayode got into their pyjamas and had showers. Theo had no clothes to wear, so Vaney kindly gave him Roger's pyjamas. Theo found them so comfy for his first pair of real cotton clothes. "Goodnight, boys," Vaney said, tucking them all in bed. 'Goodnight,' they all said back. Roger and Kayode fell asleep right after Vaney turned the lights off and left the room, but Theo couldn't sleep. He was too happy to sleep in a real bed and not on the pavement with blankets. Eventually, Theo did fall asleep because he was too tired to stay awake.

It was the next dull morning, and Theo woke up excited to start the day. "Good morning," Mama said. "Morning," Theo said. Hello, Theo. What would you like for breakfast?" Vaney questioned. "Uhm. May I have some toast, please?" Theo said. "Of course. What do you want on it?" Vaney said. "May I have butter on it, please?" Theo said. While Vaney made breakfast, Theo sat on the sofa and read a book. Mama and Pappi sat on the couch reading newspapers, Roger and Kayode sat on the table with their tablets, eating breakfast, Patrick was at work, and Vaney was making breakfast and caring for the house. When Theo's food was finally ready, he gulped it down as if he had never eaten before, and then Theo went back to reading his book.

"Theo, do you mind going down the street and getting a sleeping bag for Patrick since you stole his space in the bed?" Ma growled. Theo didn't want to annoy her even more, so he agreed. "Sure, I'll go," he said quickly. "Great. Here's some money to pay for it. Off you go then".

Chapter 2

Stranded in the Forest

Theo had finally arrived at the street where he had spent several years of his life, and as he walked down the familiar path, he felt a wave of nostalgia wash over him. He couldn't help but think about all the good times he had spent in that place. However, he couldn't dwell on those thoughts for too long as he had an urgent task. Theo was looking for a store that sold sleeping bags, and he searched the street intently, scanning the shops and buildings for any sign indicating the store's presence.

The cold wind pierced his clothes, and he shivered with every step. Despite his efforts, he couldn't locate the store he was looking for, so he headed to the nearby multipurpose supermarket. Upon entering the massive store, Theo was amazed by its sheer variety of products. The shelves had everything needed, from clothes and shoes to food, accessories, blankets, and kitchen appliances. He felt a flicker of hope as he began his search anew, hoping to find the sleeping bag he desperately needed.

Theo stepped inside the supermarket, feeling lost in the vastness of the store. His mission was to find a sleeping bag, but he needed help figuring out where to begin. He stopped a kind-looking man and politely asked for help. The man kindly directed him to the second-to-last aisle on the left. As Theo walked down the aisle, his eyes scanned the shelves filled with sleeping bags of every colour imaginable: pink, blue, black, red, and even some with intricate designs. The variety awakened him, but he knew he needed to choose quickly. Theo picked up a plain black sleeping bag and self-paid for it before leaving the store. As he stepped outside, a sense of freedom washed over him. This was the longest he had ever travelled, having spent most of his life homeless and stationery. Feeling tired, Theo sat on a bench, clutching his new sleeping bag tightly. He noticed a man sitting beside him, wearing a black hoodie and jeans. The man's appearance made Theo feel uneasy, but he tried to smile at him politely. However, the man's response was an eerie grin that sent shivers down Theo's spine.

Theo decided to escape his current situation but quickly realised a mysterious man was following him. His heart started racing as he frantically dropped his sleeping bag and ran away. Despite his best efforts, the man continued to pursue him with incredible speed, causing Theo to become increasingly frightened. He had never experienced the pursuit before and needed to learn how to handle it. As he ran, he stumbled upon a wooden fence separating the public from a dense forest of towering evergreen trees. The sight was terrific- the trees were taller than three giraffes combined! A brown path led into the forest's heart, and a sign at the entrance read "The Woods." Theo realised this could be his only chance to escape the man chasing him. He bravely decided to run into the forbidden forest, leaving his perfect life with Vaney behind.

Theo's heart was beating fast in his chest, and his mind was filled with fear and curiosity as he ventured deeper into the woods. He had never gone this far before and regretted his decision to enter the forest. When he turned around, the man following him had vanished into thin air, leaving him alone in the dark and menacing forest. Theo knew nothing good could come out of this situation, but his curiosity got the better, and he felt drawn deeper into the woods. As he walked further, the sky grew darker, casting a gloomy shade over everything. Theo was scared with every step but persisted, determined to discover what lay ahead. Suddenly, he heard heavy footsteps behind him, coming closer and closer, making his blood run cold. With all the courage he could muster, Theo turned around, expecting the worst. But what he saw was beyond his wildest imagination.

Theo turned around and saw two people standing behind him, looking confused. But what caught his attention was the woman's appearance. She had long, luscious, auburn hair and tears in her eyes. Her outfit was on point with black leggings, a sparkling silver top, and black boots. Her face was perfectly made up, and she wore much jewellery. On the other hand, the man had black curly hair and was quite skinny, but his unique trait made him stand out: he had one green and one grey eye. It took Theo a while to realise that those two people looked exactly like him.

Theo Rovers couldn't believe his ears when he heard the woman calling out his name. "Yes, that's me," he said nervously, wondering who she was. "We're your parents," the lady exclaimed happily. Theo was in a state of shock. Everything that had happened to him in the past few days - the impending storm, the man who tried to kidnap him, his journey through the creepy woods - felt like a dream. And now, he had just found his long-lost parents? It was all too unbelievable, "Are you my mother and father?" he asked, his curiosity piqued. "I believe we are. I mean, we look the same," the man said with a smile. "But what are you doing here in the woods?" Theo asked, still trying to make sense of everything.

As they walked towards a campfire with a green tent and logs for benches around it, Zoe spoke seriously, "Theo, we have something to tell you, and I'm not sure how you're going to feel about it." Theo's heart raced as he wondered what his parents had to say. The fire crackled and flickered with red, orange, and yellow flames, and Theo felt the warmth wash over him, a feeling he hadn't experienced in a long time. What was it that his parents had to reveal? Theo's mind raced with anticipation, and he couldn't wait to find out.

Theo's world was turned upside down when he discovered the truth about his family. Shocked, confused, and terrified, he found himself in a secret world of werewolves. His parents, Zoe and Eugene, revealed everything to him- from their werewolf heritage to the potion that kept him from turning one before 18. Theo saw the full moon rising in the distance as he lay on the ground, trying to process all that had been revealed. Fear gripped him as he knew this was when werewolves transformed. He didn't know what his parents would do if he transformed into a werewolf. Should he run away or stay put? The suspense was killing him.

Suddenly, he heard a blood-curdling scream and woke up to find himself in the middle of a forest. Shivering cold, he saw a clear blue sky and many green trees. He had no idea how he got there or what happened to his parents. But then he heard his mother crying and his father comforting her.

“I can't believe we did that to him.” We ended his life! she shouted. “No, we didn't. He could just be unconscious", Eugene said, trying to console Zoe. Theo didn't understand what they were talking about. Did they believe that he was the person they murdered? Were they implying that he was not there? Theo was confused, but he was determined to prove them wrong. "I cannot believe what we did to him." "We slain him!" she shouted. "No, we didn't kill him. He could just be unconscious," Eugene said, trying to console Zoe. Theo didn't understand what they were talking about. He wondered if they thought he was the person they killed. Were they pretending he wasn't present? Theo was determined to prove them wrong. "Listen to me, Mum and Dad," Theo said urgently. "I am not dead! I am alive and well. It would be best if you heard me out." Despite his attempts to get their attention, they couldn't hear him. Theo wondered if there was something wrong with their hearing. He couldn't let them continue to think he was someone else; he needed them to understand that he was their son. “Mum, Dad, please, try to hear me out. I am Theo”, he said, calling out to them repeatedly. He refused to give up.

Theo's heart was pounding so hard in his chest that he could barely catch his breath. His mind raced as he relived the terrifying encounter that had left him shaken to the core. In the distance, he spotted two enormous grey wolves approaching him frighteningly fast. At first, he could hardly believe what he saw, but something strange began to happen as they drew nearer. The wolves started to transform right before his eyes, their bodies shifting and contorting until he realised with a jolt that they were his parents! Suddenly, their jaws were wide open, revealing razor-sharp teeth, and drool dripped from their mouths, creating a menacing sight. Their claws were poised to strike, and their pointy ears were alert, listening for any movement or sound Theo might make. As he stood there frozen in fear, Theo could only watch as the wolves closed in on him, their beady eyes fixed on their prey. The scene is surreal and terrifying as Theo tries to understand what is happening. His heart raced, and his palms grew sweaty as he attempted to devise a plan. But with the wolves drawing closer, he knew he had to act fast to survive.

Theo's long-awaited dream to uncover his mysterious past finally came true, but little did he know that it would lead him on a thrilling adventure. Excitement filled his heart as he woke up, eager to spend the day with his parents, but he had no idea what awaited him. Being attacked by his parents was not on his agenda, but it was just the beginning of a wild ride that would take him closer to discovering his true identity. There was no telling what would happen next, and Theo couldn't wait to find out!

His parents took his life. Theo stood up and glanced at his pale body. There were scratches, scars, and bruises all over it. Eugene dug a rectangular hole in the ground to bury Theo's body. The lifeless body was picked up by Zoe and placed in the hole with care. Then, Eugene covered it up and laid some flowers around that area. Zoe uttered some words:

"To honour our beloved son, Theo Rovers, we did not intend to kill you; it's just a part of our werewolf behaviour. We apologise for this accident but are optimistic about seeing you again. Love from your devoted parents", Zoe uttered. The speech caused Theo's eyes to water. He had never felt more sorrow in his life.

As the sun set and darkness took over, Zoe and Eugene decided to take their nightly walk. They strolled along the dimly lit path, surrounded by a peaceful silence interrupted by the occasional rustle of leaves. The moon was only partially visible, casting a faint light on their path. The couple couldn't shake off the sadness that had settled in since Theo's tragic death. Meanwhile, Theo sat on a tree stump, his posture drooping and head hung low. The sounds of the night seemed to fade away as he pondered over the events that had led to his sudden death.

Chapter 3

Theo's tasks

Theo had been sitting with his head in his hands for hours, lost in his thoughts. Suddenly, he caught a whiff of a sweet scent that made him jolt back to reality. His heart started racing as he realised he was alone in that area. Or was he alone? Theo slowly turned around, feeling a sense of unease creeping up on him. And there she was, a lady in a pink floral dress, a black cardigan, and black flat shoes. Her short, curly brown hair was tied up with a pink bow, and her face was heavily made up with glittery pink eye shadow and red lipstick. Theo couldn't take his eyes off her; she looked like she had just stepped out of a fashion magazine. He felt excitement and curiosity, wondering who she was and what she was doing there.

As soon as the lady asked confidently, "Hello, little boy? Is your name Theo Rovers?" Theo's heart started racing. "Yes, my name's Theo Rovers," he replied, trying to keep calm, "Who are you?" The lady introduced herself as Selma, his guardian angel. "If you come with me, I can explain everything, as you're probably really confused," she said. Without any hesitation, Theo agreed to go with her. Holding Selma's hand, they went through a tunnel of light at an incredible speed. As they reached their destination, Theo couldn't believe his eyes - they were on a fluffy cloud overlooking the city! Despite still being traumatised, he was excited about what was coming next.

"Are you ready for me to reveal the truth about your past, Theo?" Selma asked, her eyes glinting with anticipation. "I think I am, Selma," Theo replied, his heart racing with curiosity. "Listen, Theo. I know all about your family's secret - you are all werewolves! But that's not all. When a person passes away, they are assigned a guardian angel whose sole job is to guide them through the afterlife.

And here's the kicker - to enter the world beyond, you must complete three tasks that determine your fate - Heaven or Hell! Exciting, isn't it?"

Theo's heart raced as Selma's words reverberated in his mind. He had only forty-eight hours to complete three good deeds or would be condemned to hell forever. The stakes were high, and he had no room for mistakes. But there was a catch: no one could see or hear him while he performed his tasks. He had to figure out how to make a difference without being noticed.

Theo took a deep breath and nodded to Selma. He was ready to embark on this thrilling adventure, armed only with his wits and a fierce determination to do good. With a snap of Selma's fingers, he was transported to his first location, ready to make a difference and earn his place in heaven. The clock was ticking, but Theo was more determined than ever to succeed.

Theo found himself in a strangely familiar place, yet he couldn't quite place it. After a few moments of scanning his surroundings, he suddenly recognised the street and the shops. One of them, Fishmonger RUs, stood out, particularly with its grey exterior. Suddenly, it hit him like a ton of bricks - he was standing where he once used to sit when he was homeless. The floodgates of memories opened up, reminding him of the harsh realities of life on the streets and how people had treated him.

But amidst all that, he remembered the overpowering smell of seafood from the shop that had filled his nostrils every morning. It was a scent that he had never really appreciated, as it made him feel nauseous. It was like being on a fishing boat, surrounded by the pungent aroma of fish.

Theo's heart raced as he approached the dingy old shop, wondering why Selma had sent him back to this place that brought up so many painful memories. But as he pushed open the creaky door, he caught a familiar scent and a smile spread across his face. Francis, the shop manager and a true friend to Theo, greeted him during his time on the streets. Francis used to bring him free, cooked seafood and occasionally gave him money. Though Theo wasn't a big fan of seafood, he was grateful for Francis's kindness. But now, as he looked around the shop, he couldn't help but notice the putrid smell of dead fish that seemed to seep into his pores. Despite his trepidation, he had to see how Francis was getting on. As he went through the shop, he saw the homeless woman he used to share his meals with. He knew she would be grateful for the seafood he couldn't stomach. Theo's heart swelled with emotion as he realised that even in this stinky old shop, he had found a true sense of community and belonging.

As Theo walked past the shop, he could hear the man's enthusiastic voice calling out, "£2.50 for a fish! Come and get your fresh fish!" Despite getting ignored by most passers-by, the man's high spirits remained undeterred. His persistent chants of "£2.50 for a nice fish!" echoed through the air, excited Theo to try out some fresh seafood. He walked into the shop without being noticed, and the sparkling clean door opened with a gentle creak. As Theo stepped inside, he was greeted by the cheerful Francis, who had just prepared his order. He could hardly contain his excitement as he anticipated the taste of the delicious seafood that was waiting for him. Although he wished to stay and chat with Francis, he knew he had to hurry and savour every bite of the tasty meal.

Francis wiped the greasy counter with a sigh, missing the usual banter with Theo. Suddenly, a ghostly whisper reached his ears, "It’s me, Theo. Can you hear me?" Francis froze, thinking he was losing his mind. But Theo's voice grew urgent, "I'm dead, Francis, and I need your help to go to heaven!" Francis gasped as he felt a cold touch on his shirt. He spun around but saw no one. Theo's ghost had possessed him! As Francis struggled to understand, Theo pleaded, "You know me, Francis—the homeless boy across the street. I need your help. Please!" With a shiver, Francis realised he had to act fast. "I must be dreaming," he muttered.

The air was thick with tension as Francis pondered his exhaustion. Suddenly, a woman's voice broke through his thoughts. "Francisyyy! Where are you? We need you!" she called urgently. It was Bridgette, and she sounded worried. "Francisyy, are you all right?" "I'm fine, just tired," Francis replied wearily. "What's the matter, Bridgette?" "We need your help. A stubborn customer is requesting salmon, but we don't have any left," Bridgette explained, the frustration evident in her voice.

With a heavy sigh, Francis agreed to assist. "Okay, I'm coming. Give me five minutes," he said before Bridgette hurriedly left the room.

As he turned to leave, Francis was startled by Theo standing before him. "Francis, wait! Before you go, please listen to me," Theo pleaded desperately. Francis turned around, facing Theo without knowing, and stared at him.

"Theo! Is that you?" Francis exclaimed, surprised. "Why do you look so pale like a ghost?" Theo didn't know exactly what he saw but knew Francis could see him. "Yes, Francis, it's me!" Theo said, relieved. "I'm a ghost, and I need your help!"

Francis felt a wave of dizziness wash over him. "I think I'm too old for this job," he muttered, wondering what other surprises awaited him.

With a loud THUD, Francis plummeted to the ground. Suddenly, Bridgette burst into the room with her striking brown hair and bold blond highlights. Her chocolate lipstick matched her intense gaze as she surveyed the scene. Her heart racing, she rushed to Francis's side and was horrified to find him lying motionless on the floor. Without hesitation, she frantically dialled the emergency service number, hoping against hope that help would arrive in time.

An ambulance siren could be heard in the distance within a few moments. As it got closer, a small crowd of curious onlookers gathered outside the shop, wondering what was happening inside. Bridgette, with a look of concern on her face, explained to the paramedics that she had heard a loud thud and then found Francis lying unconscious on the floor. The experienced paramedics quickly sprang into action, skilfully checking Francis's vital signs, including his heartbeat, pulse, blood level, oxygen levels, and blood pressure, to determine the cause of his sudden collapse. Meanwhile, Theo, with a heavy heart, knew that he was the one responsible for Francis's fainting, but he kept quiet and felt terrible. The paramedics attached Francis to a variety of small machines that constantly monitored his vital signs and provided him with an oxygen mask as they carefully placed him onto a stretcher.

The paramedic, Bethany, with her brown hair cascading over her shoulders and minimal makeup, informed the people gathered that they suspected the cause of the man's collapse was dehydration. However, they wanted to transfer him to the hospital to perform some tests to ensure everything was all right. Bridgette sighs of concern over the man's condition. She hopes he will recover quickly since he manages Fishmongers RUs, a vital community component. Meanwhile, the police arrive at the scene to investigate the matter, looking for any signs of foul play. Theo, who was terrified and anxious, was a ghost and didn't want to be seen by anyone, especially not the police. If they saw him or conducted a DNA test, they would identify him and attempt to locate him, which he feared would endanger his friends. As a result, he watched as the police interviewed all witnesses and suspects, including Vaney.

Bridgette, who was also concerned, assured the paramedics that she would be present at the hospital as soon as her shift concluded, which would be in an hour. "We think that he might have fainted from dehydration, but we're going to take him to the hospital for some tests just to make sure everything is absolutely fine," the paramedic, Bethany, said. Bethany had shoulder-length brown hair and little to no makeup on. "Okay. I hope he can return to work soon, as he is a big part of Fishmonger RUs. He's the manager", Bridgette said, exhaling in consolation. Police were also in the shop investigating for anything suspicious.

Theo was scared that the police could see him because Francis could see him. If the police saw him or tested his DNA, they would know if it was him, and then they would try to find him. Witnesses and suspects will be interviewed, including Vaney, and the last thing Theo wanted was another one of his friends to get hurt. Theo was scared because he was a ghost and didn't think the police could arrest him even if they tried. "I'll be at the hospital as soon as my shift ends. Just give me an hour", Bridgette told the paramedics.

As Patsy rushed to the scene, her heart was pounding with excitement. "Okay, but first, can you give me Francis's details?" she asked, eager to start. Bridgette quickly filled her in. "His full name is Francis Kingsellar, and his birthday is 16 January 1955. He lives on St Lawrence's Drive, just down the street." Patsy thanked her and asked for her full name and date of birth so she could be identified at the hospital.

As the experienced paramedics arrived and wheeled Francis into the ambulance, Patsy climbed back to watch him while her partner got in the front. The sirens blared, and the lights flashed as they weaved in and out of traffic, the situation's urgency palpable. Patsy did everything she could to stabilise Francis, her focus unwavering as they rushed towards the hospital. As they pulled away, Theo was left feeling devastated, but Patsy knew they had done everything they could to save Francis's life.

Chapter 4

Crime Scene

Theo's heart was racing as he recalled that stormy evening. The rain was pouring down so heavily that he could barely see anything. The streets were deserted, except for a man across the road who caught Theo's attention. The man was dressed in all black and wielded a baseball bat, eyeing the jewellery shop across the street. Suddenly, the man swung the bat with all his might, shattering the big window and sending glass flying everywhere. Theo watched in horror as the man clambered into the shop and emerged a few moments later, carrying countless gold goods and a big bag. It was a daring heist right in front of Theo's eyes.

He knew he had to report it but was at a loss for what to do.

Just then, a police officer approached him. "Hello, sir. What's your name?" asked the officer. "My name's Theo. Theo Rovers," he replied, his heart racing faster with apprehension. The officer introduced himself as PC Olabanjo and asked Theo a few questions. "Have you seen a man wearing black trousers and a top, holding an innumerable amount of jewellery?" he asked. "Officer, I have seen that man," Theo replied, shaking slightly. "He stole goods from that store across from me, where there is a broken window and glass surrounding the area. He stole right before me, so he's not very clever."

With that, Theo felt a sense of relief wash over him. He had done the right thing by reporting the crime. The police officer thanked him for the information and rewarded him with money.

Theo couldn't believe it - he had just witnessed a daring robbery, and now he was holding some cold hard cash as a reward. It was a night he would never forget. Theo's heart was racing as he recalled that stormy evening. The rain was pouring down so heavily that he could barely see anything. The streets were deserted, except for a man across the road who caught Theo's attention. The man was dressed in all black and wielded a baseball bat, eyeing the jewellery shop across the street. Suddenly, the man swung the bat with all his might, shattering the big window and sending glass flying everywhere.

The crime scene was quickly transformed into a hive of activity as more police officers arrived and began cordoning off the area with blue and white tape. Meanwhile, the fire brigade worked with great urgency to remove the debris of broken glass from the road, aware of its potential danger to the public. As police cars and fire trucks pulled up, the flashing blue and red lights illuminated every street corner, creating a dazzling spectacle that could quickly leave a person breathless. Despite the danger, Theo bravely crossed the road and sneaked into the sealed-off shop to assess the extent of the damage. The shelves and tables had been emptied, and broken glass was scattered across the floor. Theo, who had removed his shoes earlier, was forced to tread carefully to avoid the glass shards that littered the ground. With each step, he risked receiving minor cuts on the back of his feet.

PC Olabanjo's booming voice suddenly shattered the silence, causing Theo to jump in fright. "Oi! Young lad! What are you doing here?" the officer demanded. Theo's heart raced with fear and stuttered, "I... uh...I'm sorry, officer. Please don't send me to jail!" "I don't think you understand, son," PC Olabanjo said, slightly confused. "Yes, I know. I'm not very educated, but my friend Vaney sees me four or five times a week and brings books to teach me. She's very kind," Theo said, trying to explain. "That's very nice, Mr. Rovers, but you're not allowed to be here. Do you understand why?" PC Olabanjo asked. "Umm, is it because the shop is closed to the public with tape?" Theo asked uncertainly.

Theo stood frozen in front of PC Olabanjo, realising the severity of his actions. "Next time, please think before you act. It could get you into serious trouble, especially if the police are involved," PC Olabanjo warned sternly. As he left the shop, Theo nodded, ashamed and embarrassed. He tried to forget the incident, but then a woman wearing a nightgown sprinted into the shop with a panicked look. Theo's curiosity was piqued, and he wondered who this woman could be and what had happened to her. The air was tense, and Theo couldn't help but feel that something big was about to happen.

"Good evening, officer! You got to help me! My heart is pounding out of my chest!" exclaimed Gweneth Armstrong, the owner of a small shop in the downtown area. "I was fast asleep when I heard a loud crash followed by shattering glass. I quickly checked my security cameras and noticed an intruder walking in and stealing all of my valuable possessions. I rushed here as fast as I could and was about to call the cops when I saw you guys pull up. Please, you've got to catch the thief and bring them to justice - I can't believe someone would do something so ruthless!" Claire pleaded with PC Olabanjo, who reassured her by saying, "Don't worry, we've got this covered. Our team is already on the case, and we'll do everything in our power to catch the culprit and bring them to justice."

Claire's heart was racing as she wiped the sweat from her forehead. "I don't think I'll be able to sleep tonight," she murmured, her voice trembling with fear. The police officer, PC Olabanjo, looked at her with a reassuring smile. "Don't worry, Madam. You're safe now." But Claire needed to be convinced. "Should I stay here then?" she asked, her eyes darting nervously. PC Olabanjo shook his head. "No, it's best if you get some rest. We'll call you in the morning, and you can return then." Claire nodded and walked away, her mind racing about what had happened. As she climbed into her car and drove off slowly, Theo, a homeless boy she had often lectured, overheard everything. Claire had always thought he was faking his homelessness. "Stop pretending! No one buys your act. Your cup is almost empty, faker!" Claire sneered. But Theo didn't let her ruin his day. He remembered Vaney's advice: let the haters hate and keep moving forward. A small part of him was secretly glad that Claire was the one who tried to bring him down. It felt like karma for all the times she had been rude. Theo decided to turn this negative experience into a positive one and let it fuel his determination to succeed. But now she realised she might have been wrong. The night was full of danger and uncertainty, and Claire knew she would never forget it.

PC Onabanjo's voice was urgent over the walkie-talkie, "We have a criminal on the loose! He stole expensive jewellery from Quays Jewellers on The High Street."

The operator quickly responded, "Do you know which direction the suspect is headed?"

PC Olabanjo replied, "We have a witness to the crime - Theo Rovers, the homeless boy who sits across the shop. I'm going to ask him a few questions."

As he approached Theo, the boy was trembling with fear. "Hello, Theo. You are a key witness to a crime. I need to ask you a couple of questions," he said.

Theo nervously replied, "Okay, but I don't want to go to jail."

PC Olabanjo reassured him, "Don't worry, witnesses don't go to jail unless they helped commit the crime. Now tell me, what direction did the criminal go?"

"He went to the left and ran straight ahead. If you want to see exactly where he went, you can check the street cameras. There's one on every two street lights. So you can check those if you want," Theo explained.

Excitement filled the air as PC Olabanjo relayed the information to the operator. "We'll check the cameras, Theo. Do you know what the suspect was wearing?" he asked, determined to catch the criminal.

The night was pitch black as shattered glass echoed through the deserted streets. Quays Jewellers lay in ruins as the burglar made off with all the precious treasures he could carry in his black bag. Fortunately, PC Olabanjo arrived on the scene quickly and interviewed a witness, Theo Rovers, who provided valuable information about the thief's appearance and the direction in which he ran off. The police wasted no time accessing the street cameras and confirmed the thief's escape route. However, the real breakthrough came when they discovered that the store owner, Claire Walters, had security cameras installed inside the shop. With her help, the footage was quickly retrieved, and the police were able to identify the thief's face.

A search was launched, and the thief was caught and brought to justice. Claire's shop was cleaned, and all the stolen jewellery was returned to its rightful place. The insurance even funded the repairs to the broken window, ensuring that Claire's business was back up and running quickly. Theo couldn't believe he had been involved in such an exciting and dangerous situation. He was relieved that he wasn't in trouble with the police and was thrilled to have played a small part in helping to catch the burgla

Chapter 5

Mission Impossible

Theo's heart was racing as he stumbled out of the dingy shop. Suddenly, his guardian angel, Selma, appeared out of nowhere and delivered some terrifying news - he was one step closer to hell! Theo had already sent his best friend to the hospital, and he had two more tasks to complete. If they were terrible, he would be doomed for sure. But if he managed to do one good deed, he would have a chance at heaven.

Theo was terrified, but Selma tempted him with promises of a fantastical world beyond his wildest dreams. Despite his fear, Theo stood and pledged to try his best. Selma sent him off for his next task, and Theo was transported through a tunnel of blinding light in the blink of an eye.

When he opened his eyes, he found himself standing in a place beyond his wildest imagination. It was like nothing he had ever seen, and he couldn't believe his eyes. What was this strange place, and what was his next task? Theo's heart was pounding with excitement and fear as he prepared to embark on his next adventure.

The forest was bursting with life, with the rustling of leaves and the sweet melodies of chirping birds filling the air. Theo stood in awe, looking up at the towering evergreen trees and their branches stretching endlessly towards the sky. A narrow, gritty path caught his attention as he gazed ahead, beckoning him to explore the unknown. With a sense of adventure surging through his veins, Theo followed the path, eager to see what awaited him.

Suddenly, a soft and familiar voice drifted towards him, asking if he was right and suggesting a one-year memorial for someone. Theo's heart pounded with excitement as he recognised the voice and continued towards it.

As he emerged into a clearing, he saw a roaring bonfire casting flickering shadows across the faces of a man and a woman. He could only see the back of their heads but felt a rush of anticipation. Could it be who he thought it was? As he circled the fire, he caught a glimpse of their faces. It was his parents! Theo's heart leapt with joy at the sight of them. The warmth of the fire, the crackling flames, and the sight of his parents made Theo feel like he was finally home.

"You won't believe it's already been a year since he passed away, and it wasn't even due to a medical condition but because of our wild animal instincts!" exclaimed Zoe. Theo was taken aback as he had thought it had only been a couple of days since his death. The realisation hit him like a ton of bricks, and he knew he had to get to the bottom of this mystery. Theo's voice echoed through the empty house as he yelled for Selma. He had something significant to ask her, and he needed her help. Suddenly, out of nowhere, Selma appeared before him, ready to assist.

"What's going on, Theo?" Selma asked, sensing the urgency in his voice.

“My parents are saying it's been a year since I died, but it's only been a couple of days, right?" Theo blurted out, his heart pounding in his chest.

Selma's expression turned to concern as she explained the truth to him. "When you die, the timing works differently. You need to understand that from the moment your soul leaves your body, time becomes irrelevant." Theo was in shock. "Wow, I can't believe that happened. I never suspected that." As Selma vanished from the woods, Theo turned to face his parents, tears streaming down his face. He saw a bundle of flowers and candles arranged in a rectangular shape next to them, and he instantly knew that it was his burial site. Overwhelmed with emotion, Theo began to cry, realising that his life would never be the same again.

It was almost nightfall, and Theo knew he needed to act fast. He had less than a day to complete his mission. "Mum! Dad! Please respond!" Theo begged, but they didn't seem to hear him. Zoe wiped away a tear and thought, "I wish we hadn't turned into werewolves on the night our Theo needed us the most." Theo's hope began to fade as he called again, "Mum! Dad! Please give me a sign if you can hear me." At that moment, Theo's dad looked up and saw him. His face lit up, and Theo felt a sudden wave of relief. "Zoe! Zoe! Look up! Look who it is!" Eugene exclaimed, nudging Zoe. Zoe followed his gaze and shouted out, "Theo? Is that you?" "Yes, it's me, your werewolf son!" replied Theo happily. "Can you see me?" "Yes, we can see you, but you look slightly faded and shiny," said Eugene. "That's because I am a ghost," Theo explained. Eugene gasped in shock, and Theo felt a sense of wonder.

"I need to complete three tasks to decide whether I go to heaven or hell," Theo explained as Zoe interrogated him. "I have already done one task, and it was bad. I sent Francis Kingsellar to the hospital, so I am one step closer to going to hell. I need your help to complete my second task." Zoe was shocked to hear this. "Oh my goodness! I can't believe that.

Of course, we will help you and know your next task exactly. However, we want to apologise to you. We never intended to harm you. It was our werewolf forms that made us go savage. If we had one wish, it would be to bring you back alive."

Theo was grateful for their apology. "That's okay. I know you wouldn't do it on purpose, but what is my task?" Eugene hesitated before saying, "There's no easy way to say it, but your next job is to...kill us!" Theo went blank. He had already been through so much trauma these past few days, and he certainly wasn't ready for this. Theo's eyes widened in disbelief as he exclaimed, "What? No way am I doing that." His heart raced as he struggled to comprehend the danger that lay ahead. "Why do you want to be killed?" he asked in utter shock, bracing himself for the unexpected and thrilling adventure that awaited him.

Zoe's voice trembled with fear as she requested, "We need to join you in the afterlife, but we didn't know there would be impossible tasks to accomplish. We werewolves can't end our lives ourselves; we were made to destroy, not to be destroyed. But then you came along, and we knew you were the only one who could help us." Theo was stunned by the sudden plea and tried to convince them otherwise, "No! Please don't do this for me. Although we haven't seen each other in thirteen years, we will be reunited in a few decades." But Eugene interrupted with a firm voice, "No, Theo. We've already made up our minds. We are determined to achieve this goal." He made it clear that no arguments would change their decision. Theo's mind raced as he stayed silent for a few moments. Finally, he spoke up again.

"Theo, we have only one option left," Eugene exclaimed urgently. "There's a store on the

High street that sells guns only to authorised personnel. Mpho, the owner of the shop, is an old friend of mine. He's trustworthy and has a robust security system in place. He checks people's identification before selling them anything. You can even book an appointment to buy from his shop. And the good news is nobody can see you since you're a ghost. The store is called Trigger, and it's close to the place where you used to sit. If you go right from there, you'll see the shop right before you. You should see some guns hanging from the wall through the windows. The shop is open for another half an hour, so hurry. We can't afford to waste any more time, Theo."

Theo's eyes widened with excitement as Eugene wrapped up his lengthy speech. "Okay, I think I've got it," he exclaimed eagerly. "Should I go now?" Without hesitation, Zoe chimed in, her voice brimming with enthusiasm. "Go now and know that we have always loved you, Theo - and always will!" With a soft smile, Theo nodded his agreement and followed the winding path out of the dense forest, his heart racing with anticipation for the adventures that awaited him. The night had fallen, and eerie and shadowy trees surrounded Theo. The rustling leaves and creaking branches only added to the moment's thrill. As he hurried along the stony path, his heart was racing with excitement and anticipation of what was to come—shooting his parents in just a few hours. It all felt surreal, like something out of an action-packed thriller. He had never imagined that he would take such drastic steps.

The High Street was mainly deserted, and the closed shops only added to the mystery of the night. However, a bright light shone through the window of one open store in the distance, casting a warm glow on the pavement. Theo recognised it as the Trigger shop, and his adrenaline spiked. He felt as nervous and jittery as he did when he encountered the police after Gweneth Armstrong's shop got robbed. As he walked closer, he saw someone come out of the shop carrying a large gun and looking happy, which only added to his excitement. Finally, Theo reached the shop, took a deep breath, and walked inside. The store walls were a dull grey, and the various types of guns hanging from them sent shivers down his spine. But he was determined to get what he needed to make his plan successful. The weapons ranged from small flare guns to large and intimidating rifles, and Theo was amazed and thrilled by what he saw. It was like being in a movie!

Theo knew he had to act quickly and decisively to pull this off. He picked out the perfect weapon and left the shop, his heart beating with excitement and anticipation. The night was his ally, and he knew he was about to make history. As soon as Theo entered the gun shop, he could sense something was off. The store owner, Mpho, was busy selling guns to three men in grey camouflage combat uniforms - all soldiers. Theo couldn't help but think that risking your life at such a young age was a waste, especially when there were so many other jobs in the world. The man at the front of the queue asked too many questions, fumbling to find his ID, while the other two were getting restless by the minute. Not wanting to get caught up in trouble, Theo quickly found a wooden chair to sit on, hoping the shop would close soon. Who knows what could happen in a place like this?

Chapter 6

Risk Taking

Mpho, the manager of the local weapons store, was confronted by a man who demanded the newest and most lethal rifle he had, claiming that it was urgently needed for the army. But Mpho, a strict law abider, requested the man's ID, which the man, named Drew Winters, refused to produce, throwing a tantrum and insisting that he was known to Mpho. However, Mpho wouldn't budge and threatened to call security to escort the unruly customer out of the store. Drew's pal, Sean Tibbs, tried to calm him down, persuading him to comply with Mpho's request. Drew, feeling humiliated, finally pulled out his wallet and handed over his

ID, which Mpho thoroughly examined before selling him the newest rifle for £1054.

Drew was fuming with anger at the high price he was charged, believing it to be only £100, as Sean had misled him. Sean then revealed his cruel trick, pushing Drew's irritation to its limits. Nevertheless, Drew reluctantly paid for the rifle with his credit card, still seething angrily as he left the store. He waited outside for Sean, looking forward to returning to their barracks for the training session, but his mind was filled with frustration and resentment.

With time running out, Theo's heart raced as he scanned the store walls for the perfect weapon. Adrenaline pumping through his veins, he searched high and low for something small yet powerful enough to do the job. Suddenly, his gaze locked onto a small, silver pistol gleaming just out of his reach as if calling him to come and use it. With a surge of excitement coursing through him, Theo knew this was the moment he had been waiting for. Grabbing a chair, he scrambled up to reach the pistol, his hands shaking with trepidation as he took a tight grip. This was his chance to prove himself, to show his parents what he was made of. With a deep breath, Theo prepared himself for the challenge ahead. The clock was ticking, and he couldn't afford to waste a second.

Mpho suddenly plunged the store into darkness and flung the door open, catching Theo off guard. Panicking, Theo made a run for it, but it was too late. In a flash, Mpho had darted to the other side of the door and locked it shut. Theo's face smacked into the glass, and he was left with a throbbing red bump on his forehead. He felt trapped, alone and helpless. Every breath he took felt like a burden as he tried to process what had just happened. Theo dared not move, fearing that the store alarm might go off. The silence was unbearable. But then, Theo took a deep breath, gathered his courage and stretched his arms, reaching for the sky. The alarms didn't trigger. He was safe, for now. But how was he going to escape? Theo was weaker than a worm, and he knew it. He couldn't break the glass, and even if he could, he couldn't bear the thought of walking across the shattered pieces. He was stuck, and the clock was ticking.

Theo roamed the eerie shop, his heart pounding with fear and uncertainty. He was alone, with no one to turn to for help. His mind was racing, trying to devise a plan to escape this dangerous place. But then, something caught his eye – a gun! Without a second thought, he picked it up and loaded it with ammunition. With the gun in one hand and determination in his heart, he aimed it towards the door and fired. The bullet pierced through the air like a predator, shattering the glass into pieces and creating a hole in the door. Theo repeated these four more times, making the hole big enough for him to crawl through.

Now was the moment of truth. Theo took a deep breath and stepped onto the glass-covered floor, trying to avoid the sharp shards as much as possible. But despite his best efforts, he stepped on a piece of glass. He braced himself for the pain, but to his amazement, he felt nothing! He couldn't believe it - he must be a ghost! With a newfound confidence, Theo made his way through the hole, feeling alive like never before.

Theo had barely escaped from Trigger, but he couldn't stop now. He ran like the wind through the busy streets, past the shops and houses, until he reached Fishmonger RUs. The memories flooded back, and he shuddered. But he couldn't stop, not when he was so close. He pushed on past Quays' Jewellers, where he had a run-in with the police, and his heart raced as he remembered the danger he had faced.

Finally, he reached the Woods. He stood in the same spot where he had once made a fateful decision and knew he had to keep moving forward. He followed the stony path deep into the Woods, his senses heightened by the scent of smoke and the crackle of a bonfire. And then, he saw it. The fire blazed bright, a beacon in the darkness. It was his parents' signal, and he knew he was getting close. With his gun and ammo in the other, he steeled himself for what was to come.

He approached his parents from behind, their faces bathed in the fire's flickering light. Everything was about to change, and Theo didn't know what would happen next. But he knew he had to take the risk. The fate of his parents rested in his hands, and he was ready to do whatever it took to please them.

Theo excitably approached his parents, holding a gun, causing his parents to flinch in surprise. "Mum, Dad, I'm back with the gun!" he declared, his heart pounding in his chest. Zoe jumped from her seat, relieved to see her son safe and sound. "Which one did you get?" Eugene asked eagerly, his eyes fixed on the weapon. "I think it's a pistol," Theo replied, shaking slightly. Zoe asked if he had loaded it with ammo, and he confirmed he had. Zoe was stunned. "Wow, Theo. I had no idea you were capable of this," she said, her voice filled with pride and sadness. Theo understood her conflicting emotions but couldn't dwell on them now.

Eugene asked Theo how he felt about the situation, and Theo admitted that he didn't want to do it, but he felt like he had no choice. His parents tried reassuring him, but Theo knew he had to see this through. "I have to do it. If I bail out, I will unquestionably go to hell. I need to try at least," he said, his determination shining through. Zoe and Eugene nodded in agreement but reminded him that he could back out at any time if he changed his mind. Theo promised to keep them informed, but he knew that he couldn't afford to show any weakness. He had to be strong for himself and his parents.

"Should I aim it towards you then?" Nervously, Theo asked.

Eugene answered with uneasiness. Theo believed that shooting was the only option now. Eugene and Zoe argued over who should go first while standing side by side. Despite the discomfort, Theo stood waiting for them to stop their argument.

"Guys! Come on. Let's get this done," Theo shouted. His parents immediately put their differences aside and gazed at Theo, feeling ashamed.

Eugene pushed Zoe before Theo, saying, "You are the first, Zoe". "On the count of three". One, two, three.

The bullet sped through the air, hoping to hit something or someone, and eventually, it did. Zoe stood in front of the horrendous cause of death, shivering as the bullet was coming closer and closer to her. To Theo, the thought of any parents doing this to their child was inconceivable. He experienced a mixture of sadness and specialness. Zoe fell to the ground immediately, spilling blood from her body. Theo dropped the gun and rushed to her promptly, as did Eugene. After checking her vitals, they discovered that there was no sign of life in her. She was no more.

A few minutes after Zoe died, Theo and Eugene were sitting next to her pale body. Theo was too frightened to do it again. He feared losing his other parent. Theo broke the silence by saying, 'Dad, it's your turn' Eugene glanced at him, smiled, and then glanced downward again.

Chapter 7

Sunset is coming

"Should I aim it towards you then?" Nervously, Theo asked.

Eugene answered with uneasiness. Theo believed that shooting was the only option now. Eugene and Zoe argued over who should go first while standing side by side. Despite the discomfort, Theo stood waiting for them to stop their argument.

"Come on, everyone! Let's finish this task," shouted Theo. His parents quickly set aside their disagreements and looked at Theo, feeling remorseful. Eugene led Zoe before Theo, saying, "Zoe, you go first." "Counting up to three." "One, two, three. “The bullet sped through the air, hoping to hit something or someone, and eventually, it did. Zoe stood in front of the horrendous cause of death, shivering as the bullet was coming closer and closer to her. To Theo, the thought of any parents doing this to their child was inconceivable. He experienced a mixture of sadness and specialness. Zoe fell to the ground immediately, spilling blood from her body. Theo dropped the gun and rushed to her promptly, as did Eugene. After checking her vitals, they discovered that there was no sign of life in her. She was no more.

As the minutes ticked by after Zoe's passing, Theo and Eugene sat solemnly by her still and lifeless body. Theo was consumed with fear, terrified of the thought of losing his other parent. In the heavy silence, Theo finally broke the silence with a shaky voice, "Dad, it's your turn." Eugene glanced at him, a small smile tugging at the corners of his lips before his gaze fell back to Zoe's lifeless form again.

“Okay, kiddo, I'm ready”. This time, Theo got closer because he couldn't stand the sight of the bullet that was about to kill his dad. Theo counted to three in his head. In a split second, the bullet flew toward Eugene. Theo closed his eyes to avoid seeing anything. As the bullet hit him, all he heard was his dad wince. Theo saw a small hole and blood on his chest when he opened his eyes.

“Theo, I will be waiting for you in the afterlife”, Eugene whispered, falling to the ground. Seconds later, Eugene lost his life. Despite completing this task, Theo still felt guilty about it. He fell to his knees in agony, remorseful for the decision he had made.

Theo's heart pounded with fear as he suddenly stood up and let out a scream that echoed throughout the wilderness. Two cold hands gripped his shoulders tightly, and he quickly spun around to face the unexpected visitor. "Oh my god, is that really you, mum and dad? Are you ghosts now?" he asked incredulously, trying to make sense of the situation. With a warm smile, Zoe, his mother, explained that they had been brought back to life by their guardian angels for a particular purpose. "We think it's to talk to you, Theo," she said, her eyes shining with love and hope.

Theo was amazed and couldn't believe his eyes. "Why are your tasks so easy?" he asked, excited and confused." Focus on your tasks, Theo, and have a positive mindset. Think about the fantastic things we can do together in heaven once our tasks are done." Zoe advised. Eugene, his father, added, "The sooner we complete our tasks, the sooner we can be together again, son." Theo smiled, feeling grateful for this unexpected reunion. "Ok, then. Goodbye, Mum and Dad," he said, his heart filled with excitement and anticipation for what was to come.

Theo's heart pounded excitedly as he watched his parents vanish into thin air, Zoe's words echoing in his mind. What could she have meant by "sooner than you think?" His mind raced with possibilities as he finished his second task, leaving him feeling exhilarated and eager to know his future. Perched on a rough and old tree stump, he anxiously awaited Selma's grading, his heart racing with anticipation.

Finally, Selma arrived, and Theo eagerly asked how he had done. With a cheerful smile, Selma declared that he had performed a good deed, persuading the judges to give him another chance even though he had killed two people.

Theo breathed a sigh of relief and cried out in joy.

But his happiness was short-lived as Selma reminded him that he still had one more task to complete and that there was a fifty-fifty chance of getting it right or wrong due to his previous good and bad deeds. Theo tried to remain calm, but the pressure was mounting.

As Selma asked him if he was all right, Theo struggled to contain his guilt over killing his parents, even though it was a good deed. But Selma reassured him that it was customary to feel that way, and Theo smiled, feeling a sense of relief wash over him. With his uncertain future, he knew he had to give it his all to complete his final task and emerge victorious.

Theo was taken aback by the sudden flash of light that engulfed him. When his vision cleared, he found himself in a dimly lit hallway with cracked grey walls and dark green doors. As he looked around, he spotted Selma, who appeared to be a ghostly apparition, standing in front of a door with "67" on it. Selma silently pointed to the door and then vanished into thin air. Curiosity got the better of Theo, and he approached the door with trepidation. As he approached, he heard a woman's voice behind the door, asking who was there. Theo's heart skipped a beat when he realised who the voice belonged to—it was Vaney! He couldn't believe his luck.

Just then, an older woman's voice called out from inside the room, inviting Vaney to come and have breakfast. Theo's excitement grew as he realised he was about to embark on a thrilling adventure. Who knows what kind of challenges lay ahead? He took a deep breath and pushed open the door, ready to face whatever lay beyond.

With a loud yell, Vaney rushed to the door as Theo slipped into the apartment through a small opening. But as soon as he stepped inside, he realised it was the same as the last time he had been there, right before the storm hit. Toys were scattered everywhere, and cracks were visible on the walls. But this time, there was a new disaster—wet patches on the ceiling indicated a leak. Vaney's father was sitting on a torn-up couch, reading a newspaper, while her mother was cooking in the kitchen. The children, Roger and Kayode, sat at the small dining table, enjoying their breakfast with their father, Patrick. But as Theo looked around, he couldn't help but notice the thick layer of dust in the kitchen and the crumbs on the floor. The state of the apartment was disgusting, and Theo couldn't believe that Vaney was living in such a horrible condition.

As Kayode thanked his mother for breakfast, Patrick rudely asked Vaney why she was still hanging out with Theo. Upset by his words, Vaney explained that she did it because he had no family or friends except her. She felt sorry for him and wanted to help him however she could. But Patrick argued that they needed the money and were barely surviving with what they had. Despite Patrick's selfishness, Vaney was determined to help Theo. In a calm voice, Theo told her he was there, and she asked him to meet her in the bedroom in ten minutes. As he walked past the family, no one noticed him, and he quietly made his way to the bedroom. Inside, the room was cramped with beds, all covered in dirt and stains. But even though the living conditions weren't ideal, Theo knew that Vaney had a good heart and did what was necessary.

Chapter 8

For the Greater Good

Theo couldn't wait to catch up with Vaney and share with her everything that had happened since he was entrusted with buying a sleeping bag for Patrick. He knew that Vaney was the only one who could truly understand his situation, but he needed help figuring out how to start the conversation as there was much information to convey. When Theo called her, he was surprised that Vaney responded indifferently.

While waiting for Vaney's response, Theo pondered how people could communicate with him. He realised that the person he was helping had to state his name so he could respond. For instance, Francis said, "I do wish

Theo was not here," his parents said, "We wish we hadn't turned into werewolves on the night Theo had to come." Theo was intrigued by this discovery and wondered if this was the key to unlocking his full potential as an assistant.

Vaney's voice echoed through the space, "Theo? I'm here. Where are you? Theo suddenly appeared in Vaney's vision, causing her face to contort with emotion. The sight of Theo caused her eyes to widen and her lips to quiver with unspoken words. "Tell me everything," she urged, her voice barely above a whisper.

“Your mum sent me to get Patrick a sleeping bag, and a strange man followed me upon leaving. I became so scared that I ran into the woods and encountered my parents. Vaney, you are aware that my parents were werewolves who murdered me. My guardian angel Selma explained to me when I died that completing tasks in the real world would determine my fate between heaven and hell. My first task was assisting Francis Kinsellar, Fishmonger RUs's manager. Sadly, it did not turn out well, and I may have sent him to the hospital. I completed my second mission by killing my parents, but I am still unsure of how I feel about it. I have carried out a good deed and a bad deed. My final mission is to assist you in any way I can, but I rely on it to be good to reach heaven".

"I'm devastated!" Vaney said.

Wow, what an experience that must have been! First, you were left alone, and then suddenly, you were hit with an avalanche of information. It's like diving into a thrilling adventure without knowing what's going to happen next! and then you abruptly get killed by your mother and father. "Wow, that must be awful!" Theo knew that she felt sorry for him.

“I understand that you may be going through a challenging time, and it breaks my heart to know that I can't offer any concrete solutions. I recognise that you may feel frustrated or alone due to my limitations. However, I want you to know that I am always here for you and will do whatever it takes to provide you with support and guidance. I am determined to be your unwavering source of comfort and reassurance. So, let's tackle any obstacles with a positive attitude and an optimistic outlook.”

Theo was excited and eager as he urgently requested additional lessons from Vaney. With a sense of urgency in his voice and an eye on the future, Theo expressed his concerns to Vaney, "I don't have to disappear anytime soon, so why don't you give me some lessons like you did? After today, I have no idea when we will get to meet again." Theo's request reflected his passion for learning and drive to make the most of every opportunity to improve himself. He knew that time was precious, and he was determined to use every moment with Vaney to the fullest.

Theo's curiosity was piqued as Vaney's eyes lit up with enthusiasm. "Absolutely! I'd love to help you out," she exclaimed. Theo couldn't wait to hear Vaney's plan to retrieve the books from the living room without getting caught. He wondered if she had a thrilling strategy to keep them both on the edge of their seats.

Vaney's voice echoed through the empty apartment as she exclaimed, "Finally! Everyone has gone for a walk, so I have the entire apartment to myself!" She returned to the bedroom with a handful of fascinating books, her face beaming excitedly. Theo was thrilled to learn with Vaney again, as he had missed it terribly.

"What are we going to learn today?" he asked her eagerly, his heart racing with anticipation.

"We are diving headfirst into a new topic, which will be out of this world. The topic is "SPACE!" she replied with a twinkle in her eye, her enthusiasm contagious.

"Wow! What's that?" Theo asked, his curiosity piqued as he realised this would be an adventure.

"Space is the vast and infinite expanse beyond Earth's atmosphere. It's where we live among the stars, and there are eight planets in our solar system, with Earth being one of them. Get ready, Theo, we're about to blast off into a new world!" explained Vaney, her excitement overflowing...

Theo and Vaney were engrossed in a fascinating discussion about space, and time flew by quickly. When Theo realised he had a task to complete, he was reluctant to leave Vaney's house. However, he knew he had to get going. As he was about to depart, Vaney expressed his uncertainty about Theo's task.

Theo was confident and assured Vaney that he knew precisely what to do. He rushed out of the house and onto the busy main street, which was bustling with people. It was chaotic and noisy, but Theo knew where he needed to go - the bank. He planned to help his friend Vaney, who was struggling financially.

Theo's heart pounded with excitement and anticipation as he entered the crowded bank. He knew he had to act fast to execute his plan. Theo considered stealing money from the bank but realised that there were better options. Instead, he devised a genius plan to spy on someone and obtain their bank password when they made a transaction.

Theo's adrenaline was pumping as he waited for the perfect opportunity. He finally spotted his target and quickly stole their credit card. He then inserted it into an ATM and withdrew all the money. Theo felt like a master thief as he completed the task, and he was thrilled that he could help his friend Vaney.

Theo was waiting by the machine, hoping someone would use it. However, most people who came by were busy taking care of their bank details or using the outside machine. Whenever someone did use the machine, Theo would try to execute his plan, but it would always fail. Even though he wasn't standing in line, he felt like he was. Eventually, a young woman approached the machine, and Theo quickly made his way over there, hopeful that his plan might finally work.

As Theo waited in the bank foyer, his eyes suddenly caught sight of a young woman who exuded an air of elegance and sophistication. Her long, luscious caramel hair flowed down her back, while her chocolate-coloured lipstick added a touch of mystery to her beauty. Her plum-coloured nails and designer sunglasses were just a few details that caught Theo's attention, but her stunning burgundy dress took his breath away. The way it hugged her curves in all the right places was mesmerising, and the gold necklace with a glittering stone added a touch of glamour to her already stunning outfit. To top it all off, she carried a medium-sized Gucci tote bag with a matching purse, making it clear that she had impeccable taste and a love for luxury. Theo was utterly captivated by her beauty and elegance.

The bank was bustling with activity, and Betsy was in a foul mood. As she approached the machine, a man who worked in the bank approached her and asked, "Hello, Betsy. May

I be of any assistance to you today?" Betsy scowled and replied, "No, go away, please." The man tried to hide the hurt on his face as he walked away. Theo knew that Betsy wasn't the most excellent person, and her behaviour only confirmed that.

Betsy strode towards the machine, her purse in hand. She was frustrated and muttered to herself, "Ahhhh! How does this stupid thing work?" The male bank staff approached her again, asking, "Are you sure you don't need any help?" But Betsy's response was even more hostile this time. "No! Go away, or I will scream!" she roared. Theo could sense the pain from the man's facial expression and knew that Betsy needed to be taught a lesson. He knew he was the one to do it and was determined to show her the error of her ways.

Theo's heart pounded as he watched Betsy insert her credit card into the ATM. His plan hinged on getting her credit card number and PIN, but he needed to figure out how. He quickly left the area to grab a pen and paper without wasting time. As he glanced at the numbers on her card, he scribbled them down and double-checked to ensure he had written them down correctly. As she entered her PIN into the machine, Theo was transfixed on Betsy's hands, adorned with plum-coloured fingernails. He watched intently as she pressed the buttons until she hit the final button, which confirmed the transaction. With all the information he needed, Theo's excitement knew no bounds. He was confident that his plan was foolproof and couldn't wait to see it through.

Theo was on edge, his heart racing with anxiety as he waited for the bank to close. He had a plan but couldn't shake the fear that someone might be watching him, waiting to pounce on his vulnerable bank account. The seconds ticked by, each feeling like an eternity as he sat on a rickety wooden bench. Suddenly, he felt a jolt as someone pushed up against him, causing him to jump. His nerves were frayed, and his guard was up. "Selma, you scared the living daylights out of me!" he yelled, his pulse racing. Theo was on edge, waiting for Selma to reveal her news. His mind raced with the worst-case scenarios, and he couldn't help but imagine his time being up. The sweat dripped down his neck, his heart racing faster. But then, Selma broke the news - and it was good! She had spoken to one of the judges, and he had decided to extend Theo's deadline. Instead of only having an hour left, Theo now had three! Relief washed over him, and he breathed a sigh of relief, grateful for the extra time.

But that wasn't all. Selma had a secret that she needed to reveal to Theo. She knew about his past, his parents, everything. Theo was shocked and uneasy, but Selma quickly reassured him that they didn't judge him. They only knew about his life story and what he had been through, which made him feel seen and understood. Theo couldn't believe his luck and was grateful for Selma's kindness and the judge's decision to grant him more time. It was rare, and Theo felt he was living on borrowed time. Exciting.

Theo's heart raced as he cautiously asked Selma, "What do you know about me?" He had never met a guardian angel before, and his nerves were getting the best of him. Selma's calm and reassuring voice broke through the tension. "As your guardian angel, I must deeply understand my clients, including any criminal records," she explained. "I know that you come from a family of werewolves, and you are one, too," she continued, leaving Theo completely dumbfounded. "You do?" he exclaimed, impressed by Selma's knowledge of his past. "Absolutely," Selma replied with a gentle nod. "I have to know everything possible about you to help you in the best way possible." Theo sighed in relief, grateful for Selma's empathy and support. "Good luck with your upcoming tasks," Selma said with a hint of excitement. "I'll be in touch to let you know where you'll be headed, and there might even be a reward waiting for you," she added, the excitement in her voice building up and fading away slowly.

Theo felt a sudden surge of confidence. He was grateful for Selma's help and eagerly anticipated their next meeting. As the sun set, the bank's doors closed, leaving Theo alone in the empty building. He slowly rose to his feet, wincing at the lingering soreness in his bottom from sitting on the bench for hours. With anticipation, he approached the ATM, eager to complete his final task and help his friend one last time.

The machine hummed softly, its screen flickering to life with a gentle glow. Theo carefully followed its instructions, typing in the card number and entering the PIN code before sliding the card into the machine. With a soft beep, the machine accepted the transaction. A screen appeared, prompting Theo to specify the money he wished to withdraw. As he scanned the screen, his eyes widened at the amount of money in Betsy's account. He hesitated, considering his options. Initially, he had planned to withdraw a modest sum of £300, but the memory of Betsy's earlier rudeness stung him. With a sudden resolution, Theo decided to teach her a lesson. He withdrew a staggering £15,000, confident that

Vaney would put the money to good use. The machine whirred to life, its gears clicking and clacking as it dispensed a stack of cash. Theo waited patiently, his hands shaking with anticipation. Finally, the machine fell silent, and he grasped the thick wad of money, feeling its weight and texture in his hands. He smiled, knowing that he had done the right thing. With a sense of satisfaction, Theo turned to leave, but a sudden thought gave him pause. He didn't know what to do with Betsy's credit card. He hesitated, considering his options, before gently placing it on the counter, hoping someone would find it and return it to her.

As Theo strode towards the imposing bank doors, he felt a sudden pang of guilt that twisted his stomach. But he quickly dismissed it, knowing that the money he had taken was for a good cause - Vaney desperately needed it more than Betsy did. With a surge of excitement, he realised that the doors were locked, yet he still managed to enter without a sound. This was it - he had completed his second task, and a rush of joy flooded him. Theo felt invincible, ready to take on any challenge that lay ahead.

With the cash tightly held in his hand, Theo marched forward towards Vaney's flat. His legs were quivering, and exhaustion set in, but he refused to give up. As he drew closer to Vaney's place, his anxiety skyrocketed, dreading her reaction. Theo didn't want to disappoint her, and he couldn't fathom why the guilt was gnawing at him again. He was determined to finish this mission and move on, but the thrill of the unknown made his heart race faster.

Theo's heart raced as he strode through the dark, dingy corridors of the building. His stomach was in knots, and he had a sense of foreboding about what lay ahead. Finally, he arrived at the door of Vaney's apartment. He couldn't remember the number but knew he had to get inside. With a burst of adrenaline, he ran down the hall and up the stairs, his eyes scanning the doors. When he finally found the right one, he paused momentarily, wondering if he should knock. But then he remembered his powers and decided to take a chance. He closed his eyes and walked straight through the door, his heart pounding. When he opened his eyes, he saw that everything was as before - but where was everyone? Looking around, he realised that Patrick and the kids had not returned home, and Vaney was alone, cleaning the kitchen. Theo knew he had to act fast. He had a mission to complete, and he couldn't wait to find out where it would take him...

Chapter 9

High Spirited

Vaney's heart excitedly pounded as she heard Theo's voice echoing through the silent room. She saw him standing before her, holding something mysterious in his hand, and his urgent words declared that he had the key to solving all her problems. Vaney was desperate to respond, but with her family members present, she gestured towards her bedroom. Vaney's mind raced with anticipation. What could Theo possibly have in store for her? Her parents sat stoically in the living room, and Vaney announced that she would make the beds to break the deafening silence. But as she walked towards her bedroom, her heart beat faster than ever. What could Theo have in store for her? She could hardly wait to find out.

Theo pushed the rusty door with all his might, and it screeched loudly as he entered the room. He quickly settled onto the double bed and breathed a sigh of relief. But Vaney's voice filled the room with anticipation, "Theo, you're back! Did you manage to do it? Did you find a solution to one of my problems?" Theo remained quiet and pulled a wad of cash from his pocket, flashing it before her eyes. "Oh my god! How much?" Vaney asked, her expression a mix of confusion and pure happiness. "I got you a whopping £15000!" Theo exclaimed, his voice brimming with excitement. Tears welled in Vaney's eyes, and her face lit up with gratitude. "How? What? When? Where?" she asked, eager to know how Theo pulled it off. However, Theo chose not to answer, fearing that Vaney might not accept it if she knew he had stolen the money. He couldn't bear the thought of being doomed.

Theo had made a daring move to secure a better future for Vaney. He was trying to convince her that taking the money was right. But Vaney was curious and demanded how he managed to pull it off. Theo was caught off guard and lied about receiving help from a friend. His nerves got the best of him, and he stuttered and stammered, hoping that Vaney wouldn't see through his lies. Vaney was grateful for the favour and even asked him to thank his friend. As soon as he left her apartment, Theo was filled with guilt. He couldn't believe he had lied to his friend and felt their relationship was falling apart.

Theo's heart was racing as he spun around at the sound of a familiar voice. To his relief, he saw Selma, his guardian angel. She greeted him warmly, but her expression was grave, hinting at bad news. Theo's concern grew, and he asked Selma what was wrong. With a heavy sigh, Selma informed him that he had failed. Theo's heart sank as he tried to understand what she meant by that.

He asked her what she meant when she said he had to go to hell, and Selma's answer was not what he had expected. It was bad news because he had been caught stealing money from Sonia, a woman known for her unpleasant temperament. Theo's stomach churned with guilt as he realised he had committed a grave mistake. Selma's words hit him hard, and he knew that he was in deep trouble. He felt a sense of remorse but knew he had only himself to blame.

Selma explained that stealing was wrong and that someone had been hurt regardless of the circumstances. Theo felt overwhelmed, but he knew he must accept the consequences of his actions.

Theo's face was twisted with frustration and disappointment as he realised he had made a grave mistake. "That wasn't my smartest move," he muttered, letting out a deep sigh. He slumped back in his chair, his face contorted with utter hopelessness. "Why does the afterlife have to be so complicated? It's not fair!" he exclaimed, clearly agitated.

"People should have the power to choose where they want to go, or at least good people go to heaven, and bad people go to hell!" Selma, sitting across from him, sympathised with his plight. She could see the pain etched on his face and the turmoil in his heart. "I understand what you're going through," she said softly, soothingly. "But we have no control over how the afterlife works."

Theo looked at Selma, his eyes pleading for guidance. "What should I do now?" he asked, his voice trembling with emotion. Selma took a deep breath and explained the following steps to Theo. "I'll have to take you to hell and sign you in. And then, I'll leave you on your own forever."

The silence was deafening. Theo sat there, staring at the ground, trying to understand everything. Despite all his efforts, everything had been for nothing. His dreams, hopes, and aspirations had come crashing down, and he felt utterly lost and unsure of the future. Would he be able to survive in the fiery depths of hell? Only time will tell.

But then, a glimmer of hope shone through the darkness. "What about my parents? Where are they going? Maybe they will end up in hell, and we can be together again. I will be fine with that," Theo said, feeling slightly hopeful.

"Yeah... about that... your parents, Mr. and Mrs. Rovers, are going to heaven," Selma said.

Theo's heart sank. He wouldn't be able to see his parents again. But then Selma gave him some surprising news. "Yes, you get to see them one last time. We normally don't let people see their family and friends one last time because there would be too many people, but considering your circumstances, we are willing to make an exception for you."

Theo was overjoyed at the thought of seeing his parents again. Selma led him to a dark room, and suddenly, the door opened, and his parents walked in as ghosts. Zoe was crying, and Theo couldn't help but tear up. "I don't know what to do. I have dreamed of finally meeting and living with you, but now it will never happen. It is safe to say that my life is filled with nothing but misery," Theo murmured.

"Don't think like that, Theo. You have tried your best, but the main thing is to stay positive no matter what life puts in your way," Eugene comforted him. Theo couldn't believe his luck. He would see his parents again, even if it was just for a little while. It was a ray of hope in an otherwise dark situation.

Theo was going through a difficult time, and his emotions overwhelmed him. He felt consumed by regret and wished to undo everything that led to this moment. It's clear that his pain runs deep, and Zoe and Eugene are doing their best to comfort him, but it seems like nothing can ease his suffering. Even though his parents are with him, he feels like they don't understand his pain. The situation is heartbreaking, and Selma, a bystander, can't help but feel sorry for all of them. She can see the sadness in everyone's eyes and can't stop herself from crying. It's a moment of shared pain, and everyone in the room feels it.

Theo's pain was palpable, and he struggled to accept everything that happened. He wanted to hold onto his parents and never let go, to stay in that moment forever. It's clear that he's feeling a deep sense of loss and that he wishes he had more time to get to know his parents and learn about their background. Theo's life was suddenly turned upside down when he met his parents for the first time in years. At first, he felt fortunate to meet the people who brought him into this world finally. But things quickly took a dark turn when his parents killed him without any explanation. Theo was devastated that he didn't get a chance to know them better and that he would never meet the rest of his family, including his grandparents.

As he struggled to realise that he would never experience everyday family life, Theo found himself wishing for things he never thought he would. He wished he wasn't a werewolf so he wouldn't fear being attacked or putting his loved ones in danger. He wanted to attend school like a regular child, wear a uniform, and carry books. He even fantasised about studying in hell if it meant he could finally have the education he deserved.

Theo's dreams of a better future burned brightly within him. He longed to live with his family, free from fear and danger, and finally have the chance to get an education like every other child.

Selma understood his pain and reminded him it was time to go, but she could see he needed a moment. It's a difficult situation, and there are no negotiations.

Selma's words sliced through the eerie silence of the room like a knife. "Theo, we need to go now!" she exclaimed, her voice bouncing off the walls. Theo looked at her uncertainly, his body trembling with fear and anxiety. He paced back and forth, his mind racing with a thousand thoughts. He couldn't imagine what awaited them but knew it couldn't be good. Suddenly, he remembered what his father Eugene had told him - "Stay positive, no matter what." With that in mind, Theo and Selma bravely exited the pitch-black room, groping along the walls to find the door. As they stepped into the dimly lit hallway, their footsteps echoed like thunder. Their hearts racing, they made their way towards the main lobby, determined to face whatever lay ahead. Finally, they arrived at their destination unknown.

As Selma and Theo made their way to the afterlife, they couldn't help but feel a sudden rush of excitement and fear. Donovan, the receptionist, had informed them that Theo had done two evil deeds and was going to hell. But Theo begged for another chance, and Selma decided to accompany him. Theo was nervous as Donovan clicked and typed on the computer, waiting for a response. Suddenly, Donovan announced that Theo was going to hell. Theo cried out, getting onto his knees and begging for mercy. But it was no use, as Donovan had made up his mind. However, Selma convinced Donovan to let her accompany Theo to his new home. Then, they met Benjamin, the escort who would take Theo to his destination. Benjaman was a tall and burly guy, dressed in a black T-shirt with a skull and black trousers. Although Selma rolled her eyes, Theo was impressed with Benjaman's calm demeanour.

As they went to the afterlife, Benjaman explained that everyone who worked there was already dead. Theo was surprised to learn that after finishing his education in hell, he could live a boring life or get a job like Benjaman and Selma. They even had streets and homes like the ones he was used to, but with dead people instead. Theo couldn't believe his eyes when he saw the elevator made of gold on the outside and glass on the inside. He watched in awe as they descended, his nerves kicking in again. But with Selma and Benjaman by his side, he felt relaxed.

Theo was visibly upset as he began to speak. "I have never lived with anyone. I have been living on the streets for as long as I can remember." He had become accustomed to rejection and disappointment and didn't bother asking if he could stay elsewhere. However, Benjaman was different. He was polite and curious. "You don't have to tell me, Theo, but do you want to share how you died?" He asked kindly. Theo's face fell as he recounted his tragic tale. "It happened last year. I went into the woods and found my long-lost parents. But they were werewolves, and because it was a full moon that night, they transformed and killed me. That's how I died." Benjaman's eyes widened in surprise. "You went into the Woods? Did you not know that they are bewitched? Wait... are your parents Mr and Mrs Rovers?" Theo nodded nervously, unsure of where this was going.

"What do you mean by the woods are bewitched?" Benjaman leaned in, his voice low and conspiratorial. "Long ago, before Selma was born, a witch and wizard fell in love but couldn't be together because of their parents. The witch was so angry that she cursed the place they fell in love with - the woods. The wizard tried to stop the curse, but he could only lift a bit of it before turning his love into a frog and himself into a bird. Witches and wizards are immortal, so they could still roam the woods. That's why no one goes there - they are scared they'll encounter one of them."

This revelation took Theo aback. "Wow! How come nobody told me about this?" Benjaman shrugged. "Not many people know. It's a cruel world," he said with a sigh. Theo couldn't help but feel a shiver run down his spine at the thought of the bewitched woods and the possibility of encountering a witch or wizard.

Chapter 10

Trepidation

The dread consumed Theo as he stepped into the elevator, his mind racing with various thoughts. The elevator seemed to take forever as it made its way up to the building. The ringing bell was like music to his ears, signalling they had finally arrived. The golden doors opened, unleashing a blast of cold air that sent shivers down his spine. As they walked into the building, Theo couldn't help but feel the negative energy that permeated the atmosphere. The colour scheme was black and red, and the people looked miserable, emanating sadness that seemed to affect everyone around them.

As they approached the reception area, they were greeted by Lydie, a fascinating girl with short black and blue hair adorned with many rings. Her black nail polish, decorated with skulls, added to her unique and edgy appearance. Theo's gaze was drawn to her hands as she typed on the keyboard, which was soft and delicate-looking, moving gracefully across the keys. Her scent was sweet and alluring, reminiscent of a sunny day in a meadow filled with vibrant flowers. Theo found himself captivated by her presence.

When Benjamin introduced Theo as the son of Zoe and Eugene Rovers, the werewolves who had gone to heaven, Lydie was in awe. She couldn't believe she was in the presence of Theo Rovers, the famous werewolf. Selma, Ronald, and Theo all nodded their heads in response.

"Whoa! You're a legend in the afterlife! We've heard all about your story," exclaimed Lydie, the ghostly guide. "But enough about that. Are you ready to take this guy to his place?" Theo, Selma, and Benjaman nodded unison, eager to explore this strange and eerie world. Lydie informed them that the homeless shelter where they were headed had only four residents, including Theo. She handed him a pin badge with his name on it, and they set off towards the doors behind her. But things were about to get even stranger. As they stepped outside, they saw lifeboats parked like cars in a car park. Theo's mind was blown; it was his first time outside of Hell, and the surroundings were nothing as he had ever seen.

Instead of a blue sky, everything was bathed in a blood-red hue, with dark grey clouds hovering ominously overhead. The air was thick with an eerie silence, punctuated only by boats gently lapping against the shore. The roads weren't at all, but murky rivers snaking in every direction, filled with seaweed-green water. Theo finally understood why they needed boats. They stepped into a small wooden boat, and a hooded figure greeted them mysteriously. As they made their way towards the homeless shelter on Crescent Road, the figure revealed that crocodiles were lurking beneath the surface, and Selma looked terrified at the thought.

Theo asked why the rivers had replaced the roads, trying to distract himself from the danger lurking beneath them. The hooded figure grinned evilly and began to explain the secrets of the afterlife, leading them on a journey that no human could ever imagine.

The words of the cloaked figure had a chilling impact on Theo. The very thought of Hell made him shudder in fear. The figure described it as a place of perpetual mourning and sadness, where the rivers flowed with tears of humans from all over the world. The objects that floated in the air were wishes and dreams that never came true, a tragic sight to behold. However, what was even more terrifying was the ruler of Hell, Hades, also known as The Devil. Disobeying him would lead to dire consequences. Theo's curiosity about the second afterlife stirred as he listened to the cloaked figure's explanation. The figure described it as a place that was predicted to be like going to sleep, never waking up, or being in an endless dream. The eerie and unsettling description made him wonder if it was better than Hell.

Heaven, on the other hand, was a vastly different place. Even if your family forgot about you, you would still live there. But if you had enough of Heaven, you could go to the second afterlife. People in Hell faded daily, but everyone hoped it wouldn't be their turn. As they swerved around the corners of the eerie lake, the air was thick with silence. Theo saw the prolonged line of lost hopes and dreams, making him deeply sad. So many people never got what they wanted before they departed. The afterlife was full of mysteries and secrets, and Theo couldn't wait to uncover more.

"Watch out, everyone! We're entering the Crocodile Zone," the man exclaimed, breaking the eerie silence. Theo peered down and saw the scaly creatures swimming in the salty water. But that wasn't the only crocodile they encountered. A massive crocodile was lying outside a seafood shop, and Theo recognised it as the shop where he once worked as a fishmonger. Suddenly, the crocodile seemed to eye them as if daring them to come closer. It was an intimidating moment.

Finally, they arrived at a homeless shelter where Theo would be staying. As they rowed closer, Theo's excitement was palpable, but it quickly turned to dread when he saw the sombre, wooden hut. It was nothing as he expected, and he was disappointed that it was just a tiny room with a single window. The floor was hard and dirty, and only three people were sitting on sleeping bags in the corner. The bathroom was tiny, and the kitchen was miniature, too. Theo was glad to have a roof over his head, but he couldn't help but feel a sense of uneasiness. As they entered, a grumpy-looking man and two brown-haired, silver-eyed children stared at them, looking glum. It was a less-than-ideal situation, but Theo knew he had to make the best of it.

Chapter 11

The Afterworld

Theo felt a bit uneasy, so he gathered his courage to speak. His voice shook a little as he said, "Hi, "Trevor, who appeared confident, introduced himself and his twin sister, Paulette. "What's your name?" he asked, looking at Theo. After Theo told them his name, Trevor's face lit up. "Theo Rovers! The Theo Rovers? The werewolf one?" he asked, almost in disbelief.

Theo nodded, feeling guilty and ashamed. He knew he had brought shame to his family and their reputation. Trevor seemed thrilled to meet Theo nonetheless. "Nice to meet you, Theo," he said, grinning from ear to ear. Selma and Benjaman, standing nearby, said their goodbyes to Theo. He hugged them tightly, tears streaming down his face. He watched as they disappeared, along with the hooded figure accompanying them.

Theo returned to the tin cabin, where he sat in his sleeping bag, feeling lost and alone. Trevor, Paulette, and the man followed him inside. Trying to converse, Trevor asked, "So, Theo, how did you die?" His tone was polite and curious. Theo hesitated for a moment before responding. "Well, as you know, my parents are werewolves, and the night I met them, they accidentally killed me," he said, his voice barely above a whisper. He was anxious about how they would react.

Paulette looked sympathetic. "Oh, I am so sorry. That's awful," she said, trying to reassure Theo. Sylvester, on the other hand, appeared to be deep in thought. "Don't you feel sad, Theo?" her asked, his expression serious.

Sylvester was fuming after Trevor's snide remark, and his expression showed it. But then, Theo came to the rescue, trying to lighten the mood by asking about Trevor and Paulette's life in Hell. Trevor shared a tragic story of how they lost their parents in an accident when they were just eleven years old. It was then that Sylvester's anger faded away, and the group shared a moment of grief.

Theo wanted to know more about their life in Hell, hoping to hear something positive. Paulette shared that they mostly stayed in one place but could go shopping or visit others. However, Sylvester's mental health issues prevented them from leaving him alone, so they had to stay put. But Trevor and Paulette had found ways to enjoy their time in Hell regardless. Trevor loved reading and cooking, while Paulette was an artist at heart despite never getting the chance to pursue it in life.

Theo was impressed by their skills, having spent most of his life on the streets with no opportunities for learning. He mentioned his friend Vaney, who taught him some things, almost like a schoolteacher. Despite their circumstances, Trevor and Paulette had found a way to make the most of their time in Hell, even in a small corner.

The fire crackled as Theo shared his incredible story with his fellow hut mates. He revealed that before he died, he was in the middle of learning how to read and was considering taking up a hobby. Trevor encouraged him to pursue it, and Paulette was curious to know where he had passed away. It piqued Paulette's interest when Theo replied that it was in the Woods. She knew of the Woods as the place where the witch and wizard lived. Theo confirmed that he had heard about it from Benjaman, the man he had met in the elevator.

As the group chatted, the topic of conversation shifted to the Woods, and Sylvester, who had been quiet until then, suddenly spoke up. His voice was rough and gruff as he revealed that he was familiar with the Woods and had grown up there with his parents. Sadly, they both passed away when he was just sixteen years old. Theo, realising his mistake in assuming Sylvester was uninformed, quickly apologised. However, Sylvester's response was sharp and curt, reminding Theo that his silence did not mean he was hard of hearing.

Paulette intervened and reminded everyone that they were now a family and needed to treat each other with respect. The tension slowly dissipated, and Trevor announced that they would all start exploring outside of the hut, regardless of their past experiences or fears, and Sylvester was no exception. The group silently agreed, and Theo smiled at the thought of his new family. With the promise of adventure and newfound unity, anything was possible.

The wind howled through the deserted streets of the afterlife as Paulette spoke with fierce determination. "We've done what you asked, Sylvester, but it's time we take matters into our own hands," she declared, her fiery red hair whipping in the gusts. Theo watched in awe as Paulette and Trevor stood tall and brave, their eyes shining with a fierce determination to stand up to their former leader and take control of their destiny. As they chatted, Theo asked how they could tell the time of day in this strange new world. Trevor explained that the sky turned a bright crimson red during the day, gradually darkening to a deep blood red as night fell. And when the sky turned pitch black, they knew it was time to beware.

Their conversation turned to the infamous leader of the afterlife, the Serpent. Paulette warned Theo of the Serpent's cruelty and the danger of crossing him. She explained that the Serpent's castle was visible if you followed the line of lost hopes and dreams but that it was best not to venture too close, lest you be thrown into the fire pit or fed to the Souls. The smell of minestrone soup filled the air as they cooked dinner, making Theo's mouth water. Sylvester shared the horrifying story of his suicide, and Theo saw the pain in his eyes. But he encouraged Sylvester to live in the present and enjoy the afterlife to the fullest.

As they played a board game and Sylvester took a nap, the anticipation of the delicious meal grew stronger. And when Trevor announced that dinner was ready, Theo couldn't contain his excitement. The minestrone with fresh bread was a feast fit for a king. And as they ate, Theo knew he had found true friends in this strange new world.

Paulette excitedly suggested that they embark on an adventure the next day to explore the Woods and search for the witch and wizard. She believed they could reverse the curse on the creatures and positively impact them. Although Theo was hesitant and expressed his concerns about his past traumas and the potential for more bad things to happen, Trevor empathised with him and encouraged him to overcome his fear. He reminded Theo that he would have his friends by his side every step of the way. Sylvester expressed his pride in Theo's bravery when he finally agreed to join the adventure despite feeling regretful about visiting the area where he had died. Trevor believed that facing the fear would hurt less in the long run and that Theo would become stronger.

Chapter 12

Unchartered Territories

It was a dull and gloomy morning when Theo and his gang woke in their sleeping bags, ready for his third trip into the Woods. Despite the wild wind and the red sky, everyone was excited except for Theo. He couldn't shake off the feeling of dread that something terrible was going to happen. And he was right. As they packed their bags and got ready to leave, Theo learned there was no breakfast, only lunch and dinner in hell. But with his friends by his side, he mustered up the courage to carry on. Paulette, the group leader, made a pact with everyone that they would find the witch and the wizard before they returned. They all agreed, and with a resounding "LET'S GO," they set out on their journey. But as soon as they opened the door, they were greeted by Crocodiles poking their heads out of the water, looking for their next meal. It was a nightmare come to life, and Theo felt like he was in the middle of it.

As they made their way towards the Woods, Theo couldn't help but wonder what other mysterious things lay ahead. The Woods were bewitched, after all, and who knows what else they might discover. However, after an hour of walking, everyone was exhausted, hungry, and gasping for air.

"Can we eat now, please? I'm starving!" Theo pleaded with Trevor.

"Great idea, Theo. Where should we sit?" Trevor replied.

"Let's eat at that local eatery across the lake," Paulette suggested.

"But how are we going to cross the lake?" Trevor wondered.

Sylvester, always the problem solver, had a brilliant idea. "We can use that plank over there and put it across the lake." And just like that, they were off again, carefully crossing the lake on a plank.

Paulette, Trevor, Sylvester, and Theo were always up for a thrilling adventure, but this time, they decided to push their limits and explore the mysterious forest nearby. They stumbled upon a broad river as they journeyed through the dense trees. The only way to cross was by walking on a rickety old plank suspended over the water. Paulette boldly suggested that they should all cross together, but the rest of the group hesitated, except for Trevor, who stepped forward to lead the way. He instructed his friends to follow him, with Theo, Paulette, and Sylvester behind him.

As they cautiously stepped onto the plank, they couldn't shake the feeling that they were being watched by something ominous lurking beneath them. They held out their arms for balance, but Sylvester was struggling to keep up due to the painkillers he had taken earlier. Suddenly, Sylvester lost his footing and fell into the raging river, creating a loud splash that echoed through the trees. The group quickly turned towards the water, but Sylvester was nowhere to be seen.

As they searched for their friend, they saw a group of massive scaly creatures heading straight towards where Sylvester had fallen. Their hearts racing, they realised they were crocodiles, and Sylvester was in grave danger. After a moment of panic, Sylvester emerged from the water, coughing up blood and struggling to stay afloat. Trevor sprang into action, racing to his side and quickly assessing the deep wound on his arm that was bleeding profusely.

Luckily, Trevor had come prepared with bandages and painkillers in his bag. He quickly applied pressure to the wound and wrapped it tightly with bandages. He also gave him some painkillers to alleviate his agony, but Sylvester was still in shock.

Paulette's voice was barely audible over the sound of the crashing waves as she called out to Sylvester, "What happened? Are you okay?" But Sylvester's reply was weak and shaky, his voice quivering with fear and pain. "I fell into the water and was suddenly attacked by the dangerous sea creatures. Their sharp teeth sank into my flesh, and I felt a searing pain that threatened to overwhelm me. I knew that my bleeding would attract more predators, so I had to fight the excruciating pain and summon all my strength to swim towards you. It was a life-

and-death battle, but I never gave up. And now, I'm so grateful that you were there to help me, Paulette."

Trevor finished packing all the essentials and turned to Sylvester, sitting on the ground, rubbing his sore arms. "Do you think you'll be able to continue? We can always turn back if it's too much," he asked with concern. Sylvester looked up at him, his eyes blazing with determination. "No way. I'm not giving up now. We're so close to finding the magical people, and who knows, maybe they can even fix my arm. Besides, it's just my arms that hurt, not my legs. I can fight through the pain."

Trevor nodded, impressed by Sylvester's resilience. "All right, but let me know if you need any more painkillers. We don't want you to suffer unnecessarily." Sylvester smiled gratefully, and Paulette and Theo exchanged proud glances. As Sylvester stood up, he wobbled a bit, and the three of them rushed to support him, afraid he might fall into the water again. Paulette glanced over her shoulder and froze. "Guys, keep moving!" she hissed urgently. "What? Why?" Theo asked, confused.

"Look behind us!" Paulette whispered hoarsely. "There are crocodiles following us! I think they want Sylvester!" Sylvester's eyes widened in terror. "Not again! Run!" he shouted. They sprinted around a corner and darted into a shop, diving behind the counter for cover. Trevor peeked out of the window and saw a group of crocodiles lumbering past the shop, their beady eyes fixed on their prey.

As the danger passed, Trevor breathed a sigh of relief. "They're gone," he announced. The group emerged from their hiding spot, thanking the shop owner for providing them with safety. They continued on their journey, wary of any other threats that might lie ahead.

The group marched through the thick, ominous woods, their stomachs growling and their nerves on edge. They couldn't help but feel a sense of trepidation as they wondered what secrets lay hidden behind the trees. Despite their exhaustion, they remained determined to complete their mission of finding the elusive witch and wizard. As they trudged forward, Theo's doubts began to surface. "Do you think we'll find them?" he asked, his voice quivering with uncertainty. But Paulette's unwavering confidence was infectious. "I know we will," she declared with certainty. As the journey dragged on, Theo's anxiety intensified. "Are we almost there?" he demanded, his frustration palpable. Trevor did his best to soothe their nerves. "We're getting closer," he said reassuringly. But Sylvester's pain began to worsen, and he begged Trevor for more painkillers. Despite his scepticism, Trevor relented and handed over the pills. After hours of trekking through the woods, they finally reached their destination - where Theo's parents had vanished. "We made it," Trevor said, his voice heavy with exhaustion. Theo nodded, his heart pounding with anticipation. Holding hands, they ventured further into the dense forest, not knowing what awaited them. With Theo leading the way, they arrived at his grave. His demeanour shifted as he approached it. "This is where it happened," he said solemnly. "This is where I was told I'm a werewolf." He looked at his friends with a severe expression. "And there's something you need to know."

Theo shared a secret with his friends Trevor, Paulette, and Sylvester. He revealed that his parents had given him a magical potion when he was little to prevent him from becoming a werewolf. However, the potion would wear off when he turned eighteen, making him susceptible to the transformation during every full moon. He had to live alone in The Woods whenever the full moon appeared to avoid hurting his loved ones. He dreaded the day when he would have to bid farewell to his friends and live alone in the woods for the rest of his life.

Trevor asked Theo why he couldn't live with them and go to The Woods during full moons. Theo explained that he couldn't predict when the full moon would appear and couldn't afford to risk hurting his friends or family. He didn't want to subject them to the same pain his parents had inflicted on him when they turned into werewolves.

Despite their sadness, Trevor, Paulette, and Sylvester tried to make the most of the time they had left with Theo. But as they explored The Woods together, the atmosphere became increasingly eerie. The wind picked up, sending leaves of all colours swirling in every direction. It was as if the forest was trying to warn them of the impending danger.

Theo, sensing their unease, asked Trevor what they were looking for. Trevor replied that they were searching for a cottage, but Sylvester couldn't see how that would help them find the witch and wizard. Regardless, they continued on their journey, hoping to find a way to help Theo overcome his fate.

Trevor's heart raced as he looked around the dark and eerie Woods. Paulette was growing impatient and demanded to know if they had any chance of breaking the curse or if they could even find a place to hide. Trevor's expression grew grim as he explained that the Woods were vast and boundless, stretching further than she could ever imagine. Theo was in awe of this revelation, and Trevor explained that the Woods were nothing more than a myth that nobody believed in in the real world. Only when people started camping there did they realise that the Woods were enchanted and full of strange, inexplicable things. Those who spoke of these things were shunned and sent away to mental hospitals. Trevor and Paulette had lived in the Woods before, but their parents were strict, and they never strayed too far from them. Now, they needed to learn about the true extent of the Woods, its many dangers, and the animals that called it home. Trevor struggled to carry the heavy backpack, but Theo bravely offered to take it, knowing the risks ahead.

Trevor, Theo, Paulette, and Sylvester were on an exciting adventure, trekking through a dense forest. Trevor was carrying heavy backpacks. Theo offered to help take it, but Trevor refused, citing Theo's lack of strength. Paulette and Sylvester giggled at the exchange, finding it amusing.

As they walked further down the path, Theo's hunger pangs caught up with him, and he reminded the group that they had forgotten to eat after Sylvester's fall earlier. The group quickly stopped under a tall tree, and Trevor pulled out some sandwiches he had prepared before they left. The sandwiches were delicious, and the group savoured every bite in the peaceful surroundings.

Theo, who was particularly greedy, finished his sandwich quickly and asked Trevor if he had any more snacks in his backpack. To Theo's delight, Trevor offered him some crisps. It was Theo's first taste of junk food, and the crisps were a revelation. He devoured them quickly, licking his fingers clean.

After the impromptu snack break, the group resumed their journey, brushing the crumbs off their clothes and continuing down the path. The adventure continued, and the group excitedly wondered what other surprises awaited them on their journey.

Chapter 13

Sealed Lips

Theo now knew that Trevor wasn't lying about the Woods being endless. It felt like an eternity since they had been walking. Everyone's legs were hurting, and Theo felt like he could fall to the ground.

"Are we nearly there yet? My legs are bothering me," Theo moaned.

"Almost, I think. We don't know, but we know that the cottage they used to live in is deep down in the Woods. Just trust the process. We will get there eventually," Trevor said, also very tired.

"Can't walk any further. What is the time?" Paulette said.

"It is bedtime," Trevor answered as he looked at his watch.

"Maybe we should camp for the night and call it a day," Sylvester said, panting.

"Come on, guys, we must be nearly there," Trevor said, trying to avoid sleep.

"No. That's enough, Trevor! We have been walking all day; Sylvester's hurt and needs proper first aid. We got chased by angry crocodiles and only got a half-hour break. We all are exhausted, and Theo's legs might fall off. Let's set up our tent and go to sleep." Paulette suggested.

"Fine. I just wanted it to be a day trip, and then we can get to work," Trevor said later.

"Everything cannot happen in a day. Some things take time, like this. You must be exhausted, too, Trevor. You most of all need some rest. You have been stressed all day. Come and help with the tent and get a good night's sleep," Sylvester reassured Trevor.

The tent was a nightmare to set up, wobbling every two seconds. But finally, after hours of sweat and struggle, they erected it perfectly. The group collapsed into the tent, eagerly anticipating a good night's sleep. Sylvester and Trevor snuggled at one end while Paulette and Theo lay in the middle, facing opposite directions. The air was silent, but the wind howled fiercely outside. Life was stressful at this point, and Trevor was determined to find the cottage and prove everyone wrong. He was strict with himself but exhausted. As everyone drifted to sleep, Trevor lay awake, consumed by the pressure to succeed. He tried to convince his team to keep going, but no one would listen. They were all too tired and had reached their limits. Trevor realised that he had pushed them too hard. Sylvester had been injured, but he still carried on; Theo had to visit his grave, which was emotionally taxing, and his legs were numb and shaky. But despite all of this, they had pushed themselves to help Trevor. He reflected on his selfishness and felt guilty for making them work hard. But it was too late, and they had to keep moving forward. The adventure was far from over, and Trevor knew that challenges lay ahead.

It was the middle of the night when Theo woke up, and everyone else was still asleep. He heard a noise coming from outside the tent. It sounded strange. Theo wanted to know what this noise was, so he snuck out of the tent with a flashlight and wandered around. In the distance, he could hear two people arguing. Who could be arguing at night at this time? As scared as Theo was, he still followed the sound. As he got closer, the sound got louder and louder. When he knew he was near, he hid behind a thick tree, wishing he would not be seen. Theo peaked behind the tree to see who was rowing. He couldn't see any human or ghost, but when he looked down, he saw a frog and a bird.

"Well, maybe you shouldn't have done it". "Nobody will ever find us." "Someone will find us and rescue us," "Give it time, you old bag." "How dare you! If I wasn't a frog, I probably aged beautifully. Not like you, you dumb wizard." "I am so glad that I turned you into a frog. My dreams come true, not to see your mean face again." The talking frog and bird argued. Theo heard the words 'wizard' and 'frog' come out of their mouths. For a second, he thought he had found the lost witch and wizard. This would be amazing for him.

Paulette, Trevor and Sylvester would be so proud of him.

The frog was a dirty green with slimy feet and a long, pink turn. The frog was two times smaller than the bird. The bird was a black raven. A lovely, pitch-black bird whose beak, which was silver, only stood out. Theo had never seen talking animals. He knew this must be magic and the witch and wizard. He couldn't just stand there and eavesdrop on them. He couldn't let them fight. This was truly important to Trevor, and he would be so pleased if Theo found it. Theo had to do something.

"Hey. Are you the witch and wizard who turned into a frog and bird many years ago?" Theo asked straight up, coming forward from behind the tree.

"What! You are not supposed to see us yet. Are you with anyone else? Have you done the clues?" the blackbird whispered.

"I'm with my friends Trevor, Paulette and Sylvester. They are sleeping in a tent further away from here. They don't know that I am here. We were on our way to try and find your cottage and work out where you guys were," Theo explained them.

"Listen, Theo, you have to pretend that this never happened. Nobody should know our identity. But I will tell you that there are clues in our cottage, that's all the information I will give you. I will not say our names or where the cottage is, but you are lucky enough to have that hint. Now that you know, this task will be easy. Now count to ten, and then go back to your tent. Promise?" the bird instructed. Theo didn't argue back.

"Promise,' he replied. He turned around to lean against a tree, covered his eyes and counted out loud to ten. Whilst Theo was counting, the bird and frog scampered away into hiding. The raven felt disappointed that someone already found him without going to their house and using the clues. The raven set it up to reverse the curse. He was angry with himself because he and the frog argued in an open place, and someone heard them.

Theo couldn't believe what happened. He found the people Trevor wanted to see but had to keep it a secret from them until they found the cottage. Theo was desperate to tell everyone as soon as possible, but sadly, he had to keep it in. Theo had to act as if nothing had happened but knew it would be tough. He doesn't like lying or feeling guilty, but he feels both. He slowly walked back to the tent, careful not to disturb anyone. As he climbed back to his side of the bed, he thought about keeping it a secret, but he was so tired that he drowsed into a deep sleep.

When Theo woke up the following day, everyone wasn't in the tent, but he could hear murmuring. He went outside the tent, still yawning, and saw Paulette and Sylvester eating their breakfast while Trevor packed his bag, eager to get a move.

"Come on, people! We need to go. You can eat your breakfast on the way," Trevor stated.

"Chill, Trevor. We still have lots of time," Sylvester said.

"Yeah, lots of time," Trevor said.

"Seriously, we need to go. Come on… please," Trevor pleaded.

"Okay, Trevor, we're coming. Just give us a minute," Paulette said, getting annoyed.

‘Oh. Hello, Theo. How was your sleep?’ Paulette said, turning her head to Theo.

"ah… my sleep. it was… ahh… good," Theo stammered.

“Okay… good. Are you all right, though?” Paulette said.

"Me?" I’m… fine,’ Theo uneasily said.

"Well, if we are all fine, we are good to go. Theo, I am sorry, but I can’t wait any longer for you. You can eat your breakfast on the way," Trevor rudely said.

"Ok, no problem," Theo agreed. "But I thought we aren’t allowed breakfast in hell?"

‘We’re not, but Serpent doesn’t know, so we’re safe for now,’ Paulette said.

There was only cheese on bread for breakfast, but Theo didn’t complain. He couldn’t stop stammering every time someone talked to him. His mind was all scattered, but he knew he needed to get it somewhere.

"I woke up in the middle of the night, and weirdly, Theo wasn't in the tent. So where were you, Theo?" Sylvester put a question to him.

"I… went… for a … midnight stroll. I was getting a bit restless and needed some fresh air."

"Really? When I realised you were not in the tent, I looked for you. I saw footprints of a human's feet on the ground, coming from outside the tent and knew it must be you. I followed them, eager to know what you were doing, and it led to you standing behind a tree and what looks like spying on something," Sylvester suspiciously said.

"While I was walking, I was… ahh. I was getting quite tired, and I… needed a break. I thought I saw a wolf, so I hid behind the tree," Theo fabricated.

"If that's what you say", Sylvester distrustfully said. Theo hoped Sylvester didn't know what he was up to; otherwise, if he told Trevor and Paulette what he did, then Theo was in trouble. Even so, he had to talk to Sylvester; if he did know, he had to keep it a secret. Theo was getting worried and sweaty as he ate his stale breakfast. The breakfast tasted terrible and mouldy, but Theo was so hungry that he had no choice. He gulped down the last bite of his food and went to talk to Sylvester. He had to find out sooner or later…

"Sylvester!" Theo said, walking up to him. "What exactly do you know about me going out in the middle of the night?"

"I know everything, Theo, but relax. I am not going to tell the twins. Trevor would go bonkers if he knew what you had been up to, and if I told Paulette, she might tell Trevor everything. It is a habit. I will not tell them because you have been such a good friend. I know you have a good heart, Theo, and you are doing the right thing. We will tell them after we finish our task and when they are in a good mood," Sylvester mumbled.

"Thank you so much, Sylvester. It is like a weight has been removed from my shoulder. I can finally breathe again," Theo whispered.

"The only thing that makes it suspicious is when they talk to you, and you start stuttering. Try not to do that, as you might accidentally tell them the truth from that feeling of guilt," Sylvester said.

"I will try Sylvester, but it is tough. I never liked lying to people, especially my three best friends. Every time I lie, not that I have done it lots of times, I feel distressed to tell that person I lied to. It is tough to keep a secret, so don't trust me with secrets. Anyway, it's killing me not to tell them when they tell me everything. I feel like a bad friend," Theo said, whispering.

"Sometimes, to keep your friendship with people, you may need to tell a little lie. My advice to you would be not to worry about it too much. When the time is right, you will tell them," Sylvester said.

"When and how do I know the time is right?" asked Theo.

"You'll know," said Sylvester.

Theo was immensely relieved that Sylvester knew the secret, as that was one less person he had to worry about. Now, he could give Sylvester more details on what happened and share ideas privately. He didn't have to keep it all to himself anymore.

"I didn't hear that clearly, so can you tell me the full story at lunch?" Sylvester cross-examined.

"Of course, plus I need somebody to talk to," Theo stated. Trevor looked back at them with a frown on his face.

"What story are you talking about, Sylvester?" he questioned.

"We are talking about… erm… Theo's death. It was quite intriguing, and I didn't hear all of it," Sylvester dissimulated.

"Why aren't you telling Paulette and I, Theo? We would love to hear it," Trevor asked, trying to get to the bottom of this.

"Well… it's very personal… and I wouldn't say I like sharing it with many people. It's only because Sylvester asked first, and you and Paulette were busy talking. Also, I wouldn't say

I like repeating it. It makes me sad just thinking about it." Theo explained.

"I can understand that, and I guess we talked a lot. Don't worry about it, Theo," Paulette said, smiling. Trevor didn't speak. He looked at them with a suspicious look on his face. He didn't believe their stories. He knew they were discussing something too important, and they didn't want to tell him. Trevor had to get to the bottom of it.

It was finally lunch, and Theo was aching to tell Slyvester the full story in private.

"We're going to go for a walk while eating lunch. Is that all right?" Slyvester said to Paulette and Trevor.

"Yeah, no problem. We need to discuss things too about the trip, so go ahead," Paulette agreed. Theo and Sylvester walked side by side, yapping away.

“Paulette! Are you crazy? They’re talking about something that they don’t want us to know. It’s something to do about this trip. They have probably seen something they don’t want us to know about. I am going after them,” Trevor shrieked, getting up.

“No, Trevor. Leave them alone. They will eventually tell us, but for now, be patient. If it is truly bothering you, talk to me first before talking to them,” Paulette stood her ground while pulling Trevor back down.

“Fine, but if it gets out of hand, I will set them straight,” Trevor said.

“No. I won’t let you. Sylvester is coming out of his comfort zone, and Theo is new. Even when you were alive, you were still quite rude. That’s a habit you need to get rid of. You could get into trouble if you accidentally say something rude to one of Serpent's workers. Please control your temper," Paulette argued.

"Okay. I'll do it for you because I care about you," Trevor said, hugging his twin sister.

"'Thank you, brother," Paulette said, smiling.

"Okay, Theo, now that we are alone, tell me everything. Finish the story, and then I will ask all my questions," Sylvester eagerly said.

"I heard a strange noise that night, so I left the tent and followed the sound. It led to a bird and a frog arguing. When I confronted them, the bird told me there were clues in his cottage and to follow them to reverse the curse. I accidentally saw them when they didn't want to see me. He didn't tell me anything else. I was too shocked to tell Trevor, and if I did tell him, he would flip out," Theo explained.

“Wow. This is big; I know I was determined not to tell Trevor, but I think you should. He will get dubious and angry if we don’t tell him sooner. When we go back, tell him straight away. It’s the right thing to do,” Sylvester told Theo.

“Okay, but what if he gets vexed?” Theo said.

“‘We won’t know until we find out,” Sylvester said. They immediately turned around and went in the opposite direction as Theo thought about telling Trevor the news.

“‘Trevor, there is something I need to tell you. I saw the witch and wizard in their animal forms,” Theo nervously said.

“‘What?” Trevor shouted as he stood up.

“Last night, when I left the tent, I saw them arguing,” he mumbled.

“Why didn’t you stop them?” Trevor asked.

“The wizard, the bird, told me there was a clue in his cottage that would help us reverse the curse. They didn’t want me to see them. It was an accident, and that is all he told me,” Theo said.

“I can’t believe you didn’t tell me but only told Slyvester, and I can’t believe Slyvester also kept this a secret. Did you know about this too, Paulette?” Trevor growled.

‘Actually, yeah. I followed Sylvester and Theo when I saw they were missing, but I didn’t care that they wanted to discuss it without us. We all thought that if we told you, you would go mental,” Paulette truthfully said.

“So, everyone knew except me? You have only been in hell for about two days and are already causing problems. This doesn’t work if we don’t tell each other the important things we need to know. I planned this trip so that we could have some fun, but it took an unexpected turn. Maybe I would not have been shocked if you had told me immediately or at least in the morning. Because you did this, I don't know if there are other things you might be hiding. Honestly, I don't know what to say," Trevor said, feeling betrayed.

Theo's heart was pounding with guilt and remorse as he watched Trevor storm off into the wilderness, his bag slung over his shoulder. He knew he had messed up big time, and his friendship with Trevor was now hanging by a thread. But there was no time to wallow in self-pity. He had to act fast and make things right before it was too late. The wind was howling, and the trees were swaying violently as if they were warning him of the danger that lay ahead. But Theo was determined to find a way to fix things with Trevor, no matter what it takes. He had to find the cottage where it all began and unravel the mystery that had torn their friendship apart.

With his mind racing, Theo knew he couldn't do this alone. He needed the help of his friends, and he had to find them before it was too late. But where were they? And how could he convince them to join him on this perilous journey? As he trudged through the wilderness, Theo couldn't help but wonder if he had made a grave mistake by venturing out alone. But he pushed those thoughts aside and focused on his mission. He had to find the clues that would lead him to the cottage and do it fast. The fate of his friendship with Trevor depended on it.

Chapter 14

After Life Crew

Theo couldn't contain his excitement as he stumbled upon strange footprints in the woods. He knew immediately that they were the tracks of the wizard's bird, and he couldn't wait to see where they would lead. Without wasting a second, he alerted the rest of the crew, and they all eagerly followed the mysterious prints, their eyes glued to the ground as they trekked more profoundly into the forest.

As they followed the trail, the tension between Trevor and Theo dissipated, and they all started to work together to solve the next clue. The anticipation was palpable as they neared the end of the trail, and when they finally found a bottle with a cryptic message inside, their excitement reached new heights. The map was full of unexpected twists and turns, but they refused to be discouraged. Their determination grew stronger as they pressed on, eager to uncover the hidden secrets. Attached to the map was a note that read:

Greetings, Trevor, Theo, Paulette and Sylvester,

I have a map of the Woods that leads to the cottage where I once lived. If you follow it, you will find clues that will help you locate me and my lady witch. We are hiding, but I have left enough hints to help you on your journey. As a reward for making it this far, I am delighted to reveal our names - my name is Kermit, and the witch is Dora.

I wish you all the best in your adventures.

Best regards,

Kermit

The group discussed their plan while following a map. Theo mentioned that he had talked to Kermit, which seemed helpful. Trevor was pleased to hear this and wondered how Kermit knew their names. Paulette suggested that Kermit was a wizard and was very intelligent. Sylvester redirected their attention to the map and pointed out an icon with a little house on it, which he thought indicated the location of Kermit's cottage. Theo acknowledged that the map looked complicated, but he had never learned how to read one before. Trevor reassured Theo that he and Paulette had been to school and knew how to read maps. Trevor reviewed the map and determined the correct direction, and the group followed his lead.

“Let's move forward," Trevor commanded, pointing in the direction. Without any objection, everyone followed him, confident that Trevor knew the way. Even though he struggled to understand the map, they were still hopeful. Theo surveyed the eerie forest as it started getting darker and the wind picked up. The sky turned a deep red, and the temperature plummeted. Trevor and Paulette held their flashlights up, guiding their path. Trevor kept checking the map to ensure they were going the right way.

"Are we almost there yet, Trevor?" Theo asked with a hint of impatience in his voice. "Absolutely, Theo. Although the map may appear smaller than real life, we are on the right path. We will reach our destination soon enough," Trevor responded confidently.

"I see. I'm feeling a little tired, and my feet are aching. Besides, I'm starving. Can we take a break?" Theo asked. Paulette interjected, "I agree with Theo. Let's continue tomorrow." "Absolutely," Trevor replied without any objections. They found a spot of grass and worked together to set up their tent quickly. Trevor then pulled out some food from his bag, and they all gathered in a circle in front of the tent to enjoy the meal together. They ate slowly, trying to savour every bite and save some for later.

Paulette suggested, "I thought we should come up with a name for our group. Most groups have a name, right?" "Great idea!" Theo chimed in enthusiastically.

"Ok, what are we going to call ourselves?" Sylvester eagerly asked as the group sat down for dinner. Trevor, always quick with his words, said, "How about we be the After Life Crew?" The idea was an instant hit, and Paulette couldn't help but beam with pride. "Yes. We are the After Life Crew - Trevor, Paulette, Theo, and Sylvester!" She exclaimed. As they chowed down on their meagre dinner, they couldn't help but feel excited, knowing they were part of something special. They may not have much food or water, but they had each other - and their new kickass crew's name - to get them through anything that lay ahead.

Sylvester's teeth chattered violently as he trembled in the cold. "It's freezing. We need shelter," he shouted, his voice barely audible through the whistling wind. Paulette quickly took charge of the situation, trying to calm everyone down. She knew they needed to learn how to survive in these conditions, and the first thing they needed to do was to put the tent back up.

The group struggled to work together as they fought against the biting cold. Their hands were numb, and their muscles ached from the effort of working in such difficult conditions. But they persevered, driven by their determination to stay warm and safe.

They realised the ground was thick ice as they worked, making it treacherous and slippery. Theo, in particular, had difficulty staying on his feet and kept slipping and falling on the icy grass.

"Find something heavy to keep the tent in place," Trevor ordered, his voice echoing in the stillness of the forest. The group of friends, huddled together in the chilly air, immediately sprang into action, scouring the area for anything that could anchor their tent. Paulette's eyes darted around, searching for any sign of a heavy object, while Theo frantically rummaged through the surrounding foliage. Suddenly, Sylvester shouted, “I have found some bricks”, his voice filled with excitement.

"Great work, Sylvester!" Trevor replied, his tone filled with relief. "We'll come and help you bring them over here." Paulette and Theo rushed over to Sylvester, the weight of the bricks feeling like a burden on their tired arms. "Perfect," Trevor said, a note of satisfaction. "It's like faith is on our side. Put them in each corner of the tent." The group carefully placed the heavy brown bricks on each side of the tent, their weight anchoring the tent firmly in place.

"Quick, everyone, get inside," Trevor declared, holding the tent door open. The friends hurried inside, eager to escape the biting cold. Theo could see the water vapour coming out of his nose as they breathed, a testament to the frigid air outside.

The group had been trekking through the dense forest for an eternity, and no one knew exactly how long they had to go. The sun began to set as they walked, casting a warm orange glow across the uncharted wilderness. Then, Theo broke the silence, asking the others what they should do next. Paulette, always quick with a suggestion, offered to play a game. However, Sylvester quickly dismissed the idea, saying he didn't like it.

Being the practical one, Trevor suggested that they eat dinner and get some rest. They could continue their journey longer if they woke up early. Sylvester seemed to be pleased with this idea and agreed.

Theo, always hungry, eagerly inquired about what they would be having for dinner. Trevor's response could have been more inspiring - they only had bananas. This didn't sit well with Sylvester, who angrily bellowed that bananas weren't a proper meal.

Paulette was annoyed that they had run out of proper food and asked why Trevor hadn't packed more. Trevor explained that this would only be a day or two trips, not nearly a week. He suggested they could always go out and catch food if hungry.

Paulette cheekily suggested that Trevor should be the one to go out and catch some food since he was the one who had brought the bananas. Tired of arguing, Sylvester yelled at them to stop because he and Theo didn't like it.

Paulette finally devised a solution - they would eat the bananas for dinner, and tomorrow, they would find some real food. Trevor apologised and admitted that they did need a proper meal.

With a smile, Trevor handed the ripe spotted yellow bananas to his three companions, who eagerly grabbed them and started devouring them with gusto. Theo couldn't help but feel anxious and uneasy as they chewed on the sweet fruit. He was worried about never finding the cottage and breaking the curse. What if the Serpent, the evil force behind the curse, discovered their plan? What would be the consequences of their failure? These thoughts were racing through his mind, making him feel stressed out.

While observing Theo's demeanour, Paulette noticed his distress and asked him what was wrong. Theo, relieved to have someone to talk to, opened up to her and expressed his fears and doubts about the mission. Paulette listened attentively and reassured him that he was essential to the team's success. She reminded him of the night he had gone out into the woods and met Kermit and Dora, a turning point in their journey. Kermit had made them a map with a note, which was a valuable resource for them. She thanked Theo for his contribution and told him they couldn't have made it this far without him.

Theo felt a warm gratitude and pride wash over him as he smiled back at Paulette. Her words had lifted his spirits and given him the confidence he needed to keep going. He realised he was not alone in this quest and had friends who supported him. The sweetness of the banana now tasted even better to him as he savoured the moment and felt happy.

With unwavering determination, the group remained focused and cooperative, resolute in their mission to find a way to stay warm and safe. They knew that giving up was not an option, and although the discomfort was challenging, they were confident that they would get through it.

Chapter 15

Fiding the Clue

The morning sun filtered through the thin fabric of the tent, casting a soft, warm glow on the chaotic scene inside. Theo stirred, his head aching and his body sore from the exertion of hauling heavy bricks to the campsite the previous day. As he tried to sit up, he realised that he was nearly out of the tent, his feet protruding into Sylvester's sleeping area. The air was thick with the pungent smell of rotting banana peels scattered haphazardly around the tent. The other campers - Sylvester, Trevor, and Paulette - were all still asleep, snoring loudly and shifting restlessly. Theo couldn't remember what had happened the night before or when he had fallen asleep, but the tent's chaotic state and the sleeping campers' odd positions told their own story. Arms and legs were tangled, feet were in faces, and bodies were sprawled in opposite directions. Despite the discomfort of his aching muscles and the unpleasant smell, Theo couldn't help but feel a sense of camaraderie with his fellow campers. They were all in this together, roughing it in the great outdoors and making memories that would last a lifetime. As he gazed out at the red-hued sky outside, he knew they were up for the adventure no matter the challenges.

"Good morning, sleepyheads! It's an exciting day today. We get to venture out and find the cottage. I hope you slept well, but it's time to wake up now, my dear friends. Rise and shine, Sylvester, Paulette, Trevor? We planned to start early, and I don't want to rush you, but we don't want to miss the daylight hours. Oh, and do you remember what happened last night? I don't either, but let's find out together. Come on, let's get this adventure started."

Trevor was taken aback by Paulette's screaming and asked her why she screamed. Paulette reminded him that they had planned to wake up early, but something happened last night that they couldn't remember. Sylvester chimed in and assured them that they had all fallen asleep due to the stress and exhaustion of their long journey. Paulette requested an extra hour of sleep, but Trevor insisted they get up and start moving. They quickly freshened up and had an apple before packing up their tent. Paulette asked about the map, and Trevor reassured her that it was safe in his pocket. With confidence, they set out to continue their journey.

Sylvester and Trevor confirmed they had everything they needed before setting off on their journey towards the cottage. Although the cold weather made it challenging for them to continue, they were determined to reach their destination. As they walked, the icy pavement underneath their feet and the blanket of eyes on the grass were the only things visible due to the cold weather. Despite the freezing temperatures, they were determined to keep moving forward. They knew they couldn't stay in their tent forever and delay their journey. It was challenging for them, but they were confident they would reach their destination. Even though they suffered frostbite on their fingers and toes, and their noses turned red, they kept going. It looked like they had a bad cold, but they were determined to reach their destination at any cost.

Despite the various distractions around him, Theo remained fixated on the night he died. He vividly recalled the vicious werewolf attack he suffered at the hands of his parents in these very woods. The pain he endured was excruciating and drained him of all his positivity. It was a moment that would remain etched in his memory forever.

The fact that he had been homeless his entire life only added to his despair. And when he finally found his parents, they betrayed him by attacking him. The tasks he was assigned in the afterlife proved too tricky, and he failed them. He knew that he had no luck on his side and that he had lost all the support he once had since he ended up in hell.

Although he understands that his parents regret their actions, he can never forgive them.

Nonetheless, Theo remains unbroken and unwavering. He refuses to let his past define him or hold him back, and he is determined to overcome any obstacle that comes his way.

As the day progressed, the weather became slightly warmer. The sky remained the same, but the sun appeared to be a vibrant red, even redder than usual. The sun's brightness was so intense that it was like a shining golden light. The After Life Crew felt their mood brighten as soon as the sun touched their faces, and the sun's warmth even managed to lift Theo's frown despite his recent unpleasant experience.

Paulette was already complaining about lunch despite having just eaten breakfast. Trevor responded with frustration, reminding her they only had enough food for meals and were not allowed to eat randomly throughout the day.

Paulette rolled her eyes and tutted rudely in response.

Sylvester tried to avoid an argument by asking where they were. Trevor responded, saying they should be close to their destination. Suddenly, Theo spotted something in the distance and excitedly shouted, "Look, what's That In The Distance?" Everyone turned to see what he was pointing at, and Sylvester recognised the structure as Kermit's house. Trevor was pleased with Theo's sharp eyes, and they all sprinted towards the cottage.

The cottage was small and made entirely of wood, with dark green vines hanging from the roof and pretty pink flowers adorning the vines. The door was made of the same material as the house's exterior and had no window. Trevor opened the door quickly, as it was not locked, and they all stepped inside to see what it looked like. The cottage was neatly arranged, with a kitchen and sitting area in one corner, a small bathroom behind a little door, and a ladder leading to a bedroom with a double bed. The house smelled like roses and magic, and the flooring was made of wood while the walls were painted a beautiful shade of dark blue.

The After Life Crew had been expecting some magical entrance or dancing furniture, but nothing happened. They decided to split up and search for a clue, with Trevor directing them to find anything that could help them. They all searched the house quietly, and, to their delight, Theo saw the clue under the bed. It read: "Congratulations! You made it this far. Now, find the tree that is nearest to where you are."

Paulette was confused and asked, "Does it mean the nearest one to the house?" Sylvester replied, "Let's find out," and walked outside. They started looking for the nearest tree, and

Trevor pointed towards a tree with a thick, brown trunk and lots of green leaves, saying, "Umm, this one." However, they couldn't find the clue around the trunk, and Paulette felt tired. She suggested, "Can we eat lunch now before we find the next clue?" and Trevor happily agreed. They all went back inside Kermit and Dora's house to eat instead of eating outside like they did every day whilst on the adventure. The house felt very cosy and warm. While eating, Theo asked, "Do you think they will mind if we see what they have in their fridge?" Paulette immediately said, "Yes! Let's take a look." Without any hesitation, Paulette opened the teal-coloured fridge and found four cheese and cucumber sandwiches wrapped in Clingfilm and beside it was a note from Kermit that said, "I knew you were going to the fridge, so every time I hear you say that you're hungry or hear your tummies rumble, food will magically appear in the fridge so have a look whenever you get the chance. Enjoy!"

"Dig in, everyone! Kermit left us some food," Paulette exclaimed as she distributed the food to everyone.

Trevor hesitated but eventually said, "Well, it does look scrumptious. Why not?" As they enjoyed their second lunch, Paulette proposed they take a break and play a game.

Sylvester agreed, but Trevor had other plans. "No, we can't. We must finish what needs to be done - freeing Kermit and Brenda. We've already taken enough breaks."

Paulette pleaded with him to relax, saying, "Chill out, Trevor! We all need a break. If we work too hard, we won't get it done properly. We can sleep here for the night, too. Please, Trevor, put your feet up for a while."

Trevor admitted, "Frankly, I am quite exhausted from this trip. So, what should we do?" "Let's play a game."

Chapter 16

The After Life

The After Life Crew was so absorbed in their game that they lost track of time. When Sylvester noticed the fading daylight outside, he remembered Kermit's reminder about calling for food. Without delay, he urged his friends to do the same. They all shouted together, and the sound reverberated throughout the house. To their surprise, a golden light shimmered from the fridge within minutes of their calls. Paulette opened the door and found four instant pots of noodles on the top shelf and four water bottles neatly arranged on the side. The group sat down to eat their meal in complete silence, and the pots of noodles vanished within twenty minutes. They were left wondering who had cleared the table and taken care of the rubbish, which had mysteriously disappeared.

Paulette loudly screamed, "Thank you, Kermit!" while keeping her fingers crossed that he'd hear her. Theo was curious about where they'd sleep, and Trevor, the true gentleman, offered to sleep on the floor so that Paulette and Theo could share the bed while Sylvester could crash on the couch. But just as Trevor finished speaking, a thick, plush mattress appeared behind him, adorned with two cosy blankets and pillows - one for Trevor and one for Sylvester. They were astonished - Kermit had sent it! Trevor couldn't help but grin in appreciation and thank Kermit for his generosity. However, Theo was puzzled and wondered aloud how Kermit could hear their conversation. Paulette eagerly suggested that Kermit was a wizard who had cast a spell on the house to tune into all their conversations but wouldn't interact. They were all blown away - Kermit was indeed magical!

"I can't wait to start the day tomorrow," Sylvester exclaimed. "After a hearty breakfast, we'll head outside and discover the second clue. It's going to be so much fun!"

Theo smiled in agreement. "I'm excited, too," he said. "These clues remind me of the tasks we had to complete with our guardian angel. I wonder what kind of challenge this clue will bring."

Paulette nodded, her eyes gleaming with anticipation. "Let's focus on the present and stay positive," she said. "We're in this together and figure it out."

As they settled into bed, the group couldn't help but feel excited about the adventure that awaited them. Sylvester quickly drifted off to sleep while Theo lay awake, his mind buzzing with excitement for future challenges. He knew his companions would be there to support him every step of the way, and he couldn't wait to see what the future held.

The following morning was dreary, with a strong wind that was causing trees to topple over and random objects to fly in all directions. Theo woke up, still feeling like he did the night before. Although he didn't want to hide his emotions, he knew he had to pretend everything was okay. The After Life Crew quickly finished their breakfast, barely chewing their food, and dressed warmly to brave the outdoors. Paulette requested warm clothes from Kermit, who conjured up fleeces, cotton coats, hats, scarves, and gloves in different colours for each of them. The day was the most terrible Theo had ever experienced. The storm was so strong that the trees looked like they were about to snap, but they stood tall. The grass was short, but the wind pulled it in one direction. Leaves, dirt, and rubbish were hovering in the air, moving randomly and disappearing in the distance.

Paulette nervously asked, "Are you guys ready to go outside?"

"Ready as we'll ever be," Sylvester replied. Theo twisted the door handle, and the mighty wind rushed onto their bodies, pushing them to the left and right. They moved forward, trying to step outside while leaves and dirt flew into the cottage. Eventually, they all went outside but had to walk to the nearest tree. Trevor put the first clue into his pocket, realising the wind's strength and not wanting it to fly away. The wind was so strong that they could barely breathe oxygen, so they inhaled the wind instead. The sky was a deep shade of red, growing darker by the minute, which was unusual.

"Why is the sky getting darker? It's not evening yet." Theo shouted so they could hear him.

"The sky always gets darker during a hurricane," Trevor shouted.

"So, this is a hurricane?" Theo yelled angrily.

"Yes, it's a hurricane." Sylvester also yelled. "I think we should wait in the cottage until it calms down!"

"No! We don't have any more time to waste!" Trevor said, his voice rising with frustration. They kept pushing forward, but the wind was more substantial than them.

"I've got an idea: let's ask Kermit if he can stop the hurricane," Paulette suggested, shielding her eyes from the storm.

As they stood there, Trevor couldn't help but feel a sense of unease. He knew that their journey was far from over and that more challenges were ahead. He couldn't shake the feeling that they were being watched and that something was lurking in the shadows, waiting to strike.

"Guys, we need to be careful," he said nervously. "I feel that things are about to get much more difficult."

Paulette and Theo nodded in agreement, their faces set in grim determination. They knew they couldn't let their guard down for a moment and that every step could be their last.

Suddenly, a fierce wind picked up, whipping through the trees and sending leaves and branches flying in all directions. Trevor shouted a command, his voice barely audible over the howling gale.

"Kermit, please stop the storm if you can! We need to find the next clue, and we can't do that if there is a storm!"

The wind died down as quickly as it had come, leaving the group stunned. They looked at each other, wondering what had just happened.

"Well, that was unexpected," said Sylvester, breaking the silence. "But we can't let our guard down. We still have a long way to go."

Paulette and Theo nodded in agreement, their eyes scanning the trees for any sign of danger. They knew that the next clue could be anywhere and that they had to be ready for whatever lay ahead.

As they set off again, each step filled with anticipation and trepidation, they couldn't help but wonder what lay in store for them next. The future was still being determined.

They slowly made their way to the nearest tree without delay, hoping the storm wouldn't return.

"So where could the clue be? We looked everywhere yesterday," Paulette asked.

"Why don't you try looking in branches at the top?" Theo smartly said.

"Yes, that might be a good idea, but who will go up there? It certainly won't be me." Sylvester said. Paulette and Theo looked at the ground and whistled as a sign that they wouldn't do it either.

"Fine. I'll do it. You guys are a bunch of wimps," Trevor forwarded himself, also a bit annoyed at the fact he had to do all the dangerous stunts. He took off his burdensome backpack and let it fall to the ground. Trevor always climbed trees when he was alive, so he knew what to do. He ran, leapt as high as he could, and threw himself on the tree. The impact was so significant that leaves fell off the tree, dropping everywhere in that area. He wanted to look like a strong boy and a reckless person, but in the process, he did get hurt, although he did not show it. He thought Theo was cleverer and braver than him, so he needed to prove himself worthy.

“Are you all right, Trevor?” Paulette asked.

“Yeah, I’m perfectly fine. Not a scratch or bruise in sight,” he untruthfully said. While his back was turned to his friends, he cried silently in distress. After the pain was moderately gone, Trevor started his hike to the top of the tree. It was a very tall tree, so it took a long time. He quickly went out of breath. Once he was in a secured position- or what he thought was a secure position- he turned his head to look for a piece of parchment.

“I see it!” he yelled. “But it’s too far away for me to reach. I need to lean on a thin branch.”

“Don’t worry, Trevor. We will find another way to get it down. If you put your weight on the twig, it will snap, and you will fall. Please don’t do this!” Paulette yelled back.

“It’s okay. I will be fine,” Trevor said, trying to look like a hero. Without thinking straight, he leant forward and grabbed the paper's corner. He could feel the branch starting to snap, so he slowly backed away, but it was maybe too late.

Trevor plummeted to the ground from quite a high tree, still holding onto the paper. He screamed all the way, and the last thing you heard was a THUD! Trevor passed out with scratches and bruises all over his body. The rest of them couldn’t tell if he was breathing or not, but they were still in a state of shock.

"Trevor, Trevor! Wake up! Now! Please get up!" Paulette screamed as she shook Trevor from side to side.

"Trevor! Come on, wake up!" Sylvester also said. "Why did he do it? We told him not to. Why didn't he listen to us?"

"That doesn't matter now, Sylvester. We need to make him better. He can't go now," Paulette said.

The group was in shock and despair as they mourned the loss of their dear friend, Trevor. Paulette was inconsolable, her tears flowing freely as she tried to revive him with CPR to no avail. The others stood by helplessly, wishing they could do something to bring him back. Trying to understand the situation, Theo asked questions that were met with silence and tears. Sylvester explained that when someone dies, their body and soul depart and go to a different place. Paulette was devastated, blaming herself for suggesting the adventure that led to her brother's death.

The group gathered twigs and leaves to create a makeshift burial site for Trevor, their best friend. They said their final goodbyes, burying him in the hole that Sylvester had dug. Paulette spoke of the profound loss she felt and how much Trevor meant to her. She knew that life would never be the same without him, and the group would never be complete again. Theo and Sylvester tried to console her with hugs and words of comfort, but the pain was too deep. They sat in silence, mourning the loss of their friend and the emptiness that he left behind. The group knew they would never forget him and always cherish shared memories.

Chapter 17

Bizarre Occurrences

The group had just lost Trevor, and after shedding a few tears, they faced a difficult decision. Paulette, the voice of reason, suggested that they should continue with the quest to fulfil Trevor's dream. Theo, concerned, asked if Paulette was all right with this plan. Paulette replied with determination, stating that she didn't want to mourn her brother's death forever. Instead, she wanted to celebrate his life and continue their mission.

Sylvester, the quiet one, leaned towards Theo and whispered that Paulette was trying to be strong and not show her emotions. Theo acknowledged her bravery and suggested they let Paulette lead like her brother had. He also proposed that they offer her support and assistance whenever needed.

Sylvester then asked Paulette about the clue, trying to uplift her spirits. Paulette took a deep breath, read the clue, and informed the group to take ten steps forward and dig a hole. She went on to say that the plastic container in the hole would contain several things, including the next clue.

However, Theo was confused and asked, "Ten feet from where?" As the quick thinker, Sylvester suggested walking to the tree's other side to figure it out. Upon reaching their destination, they started digging with their bare hands, careful not to get too close to Trevor, whom they had buried earlier. As they dug, dirt flew everywhere, causing some discomfort to their eyes. Finally, they found a white plastic container containing several bottles with labels on them. Sylvester picked it up and examined it closely, wondering what could be inside.

After removing the plastic cover, they found a crinkled parchment paper at the bottom. This time, Theo read the parchment aloud, which revealed that they had seen the clues to reverse the curse. However, they needed to return to the cottage and search for something inside Dora's purse.

Exhausted from all the running around, Sylvester asked if they had to return to the cottage. But Paulette, determined to solve the curse, scolded and reminded him of their mission. They got up and rushed back to the cottage, passing by where they had buried Trevor. As they walked through the front doors, Theo asked a question that had been bothering him, "What kind of purse are we looking for?"

Paulette was in a state of agitation as she responded to Slyvester's question. "Why are you asking me? I don't know! Just look for any purse and have a look inside it. There should be a clue, and I am sure you already know what that looks like!" she said, her voice laced with anger. Sylvester tried to calm her down. "Calm down, Paulette! It was only a question. Look downstairs, Paulette. Theo and I will look upstairs," he instructed. The trio then split up to carry out their search of the house.

Sylvester couldn't contain his excitement when he found something of interest. "Hey everyone, I found some! They are all in the wardrobe," he exclaimed, with Theo being the only one running up to him. Paulette, however, stayed downstairs to continue her search. Suddenly, Theo called out to her. "Paulette, come up and help us search through these bags," he said eagerly. Paulette reluctantly obliged and joined them upstairs, where they found piles of bags of different shapes and colours.

"Wow, Dora must like her fashion," Sylvester remarked as they explored each bag and pocket. Paulette, however, still looked quite glum.

Theo noticed her sadness and asked her if she was all right. Paulette opened up to them and expressed her pain. "To be honest, even though I said to forget about Trevor's second death, I'm not okay. When I died, I lost my parents and the rest of my family. Trevor was my only family, and now he is gone forever. I don't know how I'm going to survive. It's like the Serpent took what was left of me and tore it apart. It's like I am nothing. I'm worthless. I feel... empty," she explained.

Theo and Sylvester sympathised with her and assured her they would carry on Trevor's dream. They reminded her that she knew what it was like to be in the second afterlife and that she could end up in heaven or together with Trevor. They encouraged her not to stress about it and to focus on celebrating Trevor's life and afterlife. Paulette felt comforted after expressing her feelings. She knew it was impossible to carry on as usual with her brother dead, but at least she felt a little bit better.

As they continued their search, Paulette grew increasingly frustrated. "I can't find the clue. It's impossible!" she exclaimed. Sylvester tried to reassure her. "We just need to keep looking," he said, suddenly exclaiming, "And speaking of it, I think I found the clue."

Paulette's eyes widened in disbelief as Sylvester held up the spell book, confirming they had finally found it. The book's cover was a murky brown, and as Paulette blew on it, a layer of dust came off, revealing its ancient origins. A note attached to the front cover read, "Well done! You found it. You found the spell book. Open page 107 and take a look. These pages will tell you how to make the potion. Do it together in slow motion," which Sylvester read aloud with excitement.

Theo couldn't contain his joy at finally finding the spell book, and he was confident that they were one step closer to discovering Kermit and Dora's destination. However, Paulette knew they still had a long way to go. She carefully flipped to page 107 and read through the messy handwriting with trembling fingers. The page was filled with a list of ingredients and magic words that sounded utterly revolting. Paulette couldn't believe they would have to use such repulsive ingredients to make the potion, but she knew it was their only hope.

The instructions on the page detailed the ingredients and steps necessary to create a magical potion. The recipe called for peculiar elements such as the eyes of a newt, blood from a bird, a frog's leg, a worm's insides, and a handful of grass. Additionally, one had to recite the magic words in the spell while stirring the concoction in a cauldron. Chant the following words: “Hocus, Pocus, Hocus. Pocus.”

"Observe the power of magic hidden in those mystical words

with your voice, let the magic be heard.

To create a genuinely divine potion.

Two strange ingredients must align:

The eyes of a newt, the blood of a bird.

It may sound peculiar, but trust the magic words!

With thunder that roars and lightning that strikes,

The winds that howl and leave you in awe,

This potion's power will make you howl.

Transform the animal into a man, And unleash the magic."

As a team of amateur potion makers, Theo, Paulette, and Sylvester were excited but apprehensive about starting their first brew. With no prior experience, they were still trying to figure out what to do and had to rely on the spell book for guidance. Much to their surprise, the labels on the ingredients were not just a joke but the actual substance itself. After turning on the electrical fire under the cauldron, they realised there were no instructions on what to put in first. Sylvester suggested they toss it all in and hope for the best, but Paulette hesitated. When putting in the first ingredient, "eyes of a newt," Theo bravely volunteered despite the pungent smell. As the bulging eyes fell into the cauldron, they were unsure what would happen next. With this uncertainty, only time would tell if they had successfully brewed their first potion.

As Theo dropped the first ingredient into the cauldron, the woman declared, "Next up is 'blood from a bird'." The red liquid swirled around before mysteriously sinking in and disappearing. The sight of it alone evoked a sense of unease in everyone present.

"We need a frog's leg," she continued as a lifeless yellow and green leg with webbed feet landed in the cauldron, evoking looks of disgust from everyone. It was difficult to ignore the repulsive image of the leg floating in the mixture, as it seemed to be mocking their disgust. "The next item on the list is a worm's insides'," Paulette announced, her voice trembling with dread. Theo glared at Sylvester, who was responsible for pouring all the grotesque substances, but Sylvester seemed relieved not to have Theo's job. Pouring a worm's insides into the cauldron made Theo feel nauseous. "Once again, this one smells terrible," Theo grumbled indignantly. "Can we hurry up and get this over with? The more we go through these weird ingredients, the more disturbed I become."

With a hint of sarcasm, Paulette announced that the final ingredient was a handful of grass. Theo breathed a sigh of relief, grateful that the last component was something natural and less unsettling to add to the bubbling cauldron. However, Sylvester raised an eyebrow and questioned if they needed plain grass from outside. Having read the instructions in the book, Paulette explained that no more containers were left in the bowl, and they needed to get some from outside. She also volunteered to collect the grass this time.

Paulette stepped outside into the sturdy wind and pulled out a handful of grass near the cottage. As soon as she plucked the grass from the soil, it turned brown, symbolising its death. The wind suddenly grew stronger, signalling Paulette to rush back inside the cosy cottage. She explained to her companions that all living things in that place, including plants and animals, would go to the second afterlife, making the Serpent stronger every time. They hadn't seen Serpent in three years, and Sylvester feared what he might do when he got mighty.

Paulette returned inside with the brown grass and dropped it into the smelly mixture, using a wooden spoon she found on the kitchen counter to mix it. The ingredients swirled around in the slimy-green liquid, making

Paulette feel revolted and disgusted by the sickening smell. It smelled like vomit that had stayed there long and rotted over time.

Theo impatiently asked how they would know when it was done. Sylvester scanned the book with his eyes but needed an indication of when the potion would be complete. Paulette predicted that it would be done when she couldn't feel any bits in the mixture and when it changed colour. Theo grumbled that it could take forever, but after a while, Paulette announced that she couldn't feel any tricky bits in the cauldron, and the colour had changed to a very dark red.

Chapter 18

Working Magic

Theo and Sylvester had just finished making a potion and were now searching for a container to store it in. Sylvester instructed Theo to keep an eye on the potion to ensure its safety while he searched the kitchen for a suitable container. The kitchen was in disarray, with cupboards and shelves filled with dust. Despite this, Theo and Sylvester searched every nook and cranny of the kitchen until they finally found a cupboard that contained a stack of potion containers.

Upon discovering the stack, Theo was ecstatic and pointed out a label that read "Potion Containers." The containers varied in shape and size, and Paulette suggested they take the largest one since the spell book and clues needed to provide specific instructions on the amount required.

Theo and Sylvester sat on the floor to sift through the pile of potion bottles. The cupboard was jam-packed with bottles of different shapes, including hearts, diamonds, rectangles, and the usual ones. Some bottles were missing, and they assumed that Kermit and Dora had used them for their potions. The cupboard was quite deep, so they both had to stick their heads in, which proved challenging due to the cramped and dusty space. Theo was coughing from the dust, and Sylvester had to squint his eyes to see what he was doing.

Paulette's anxiety was mounting, and she demanded an update on the search for the bottles. In response, Theo suggested that Paulette take his place while he monitored the potion's progress. Paulette accepted the offer and made her way to the cupboard. But to her surprise, the cupboard was enchanted, and she found breathing hard. In the meantime, Theo was getting nervous as the potion began to bubble and simmer rapidly.

As Paulette searched for the bottles, she asked Theo about the number of potions that Kermit and Dora had made. However, Theo was too preoccupied with the potion, which seemed to be on the verge of boiling over. Paulette realised the gravity of the situation and instructed Theo to turn off the switch by the cauldron to prevent the potion from spilling. Losing even a drop of the potion would be disastrous.

Finally, Paulette located a bottle with a lid, but Theo was unsure about the transfer process. Sylvester, the oldest, volunteered to pour the potion into the bottle. But as he did so, some potions spilt onto his hand, causing him to panic. His heart skipped a beat as he froze in fear, unsure what would happen next.

There was a moment of panic when Paulette noticed something on Theo's arm. She asked what would happen, and it was clear that Sylvester was just as scared. In a moment of terror, he dropped the spoon in the cauldron and put the flask on the counter. The dark red potion disappeared into his skin without leaving a trace. Suddenly, he felt a terrible burning sensation that made him scream in agony. His mouth went dry, and his throat was sore. Paulette suggested that they run his arm under cold water to ease the pain, and she quickly went to the sink to turn on the cold water. When Sylvester put his hand under the running water, the numbness helped, but the pain returned as soon as he removed it. Unfortunately, they were all at a loss as to what they could do to help him.

Theo suggested that Kermit could have warned them that it would burn someone's hand. But Paulette cleverly pointed out that the clue in the spell book clearly stated, 'Do it together in slow motion'. They didn't follow the clue, and the punishment was burning. Suddenly, Sylvester's pain stopped, and there was no after-pain.

Theo commented that this was a bizarre house, but Paulette explained that Sylvester's pain might have stopped because they realised what the clue had said, and Kermit probably heard them, so he stopped it. Theo asked how they would transfer the potion into the flask now. Paulette suggested wearing thick gloves, but despite getting hurt, Sylvester insisted he would do it and take responsibility. Theo showed concern. Still, Sylvester said he would be fine if they got thick gloves.

Paulette was determined to find the missing items and quickly went to the kitchen. She pondered momentarily and decided the cupboard under the sink, where all the washing up stuff would be, could be an excellent place to look. Her hunch was correct as she found the missing items and handed them to Sylvester. He put on the gloves and got back to work. Despite feeling nervous, he was determined to show his bravery and do it anyway. This time, a little bit of the mixture did go on his hands, but it didn't burn him. Instead, the potion slid off the glove and fell back into the cauldron. Sylvester managed to fill as much mixture as he could fit in the flask, leaving the rest in the cauldron. He pushed on the cork lid and held it up proudly, asking, "Now, what do we do?"

Suddenly, a piece of paper that looked like it had been torn off fluttered out of the cauldron and landed in Theo's hands. He read it aloud: "You made the magic, which is great, but now you must find me Dora that awaits. To do this difficult mission, find the TV remote in a high position." This was the next clue! But what did it mean? Theo asked, "It's the next clue! "Find the TV remote in a high position". What does that mean?" Paulette, who was always quick to come up with ideas, suggested they should start by looking at the high places in the house. "Perhaps we could go upstairs and search the walls and ceiling," she said. Sylvester agreed and placed the flask containing the potion on the dining table.

The trio hurried upstairs and searched everything that looked relatively high, including on top of the cupboard. However, Theo only looked at the ceiling and walls with his eyes. Not long after, Sylvester found the TV remote. "It's on the ceiling, on the chandelier. The clue is in the middle of the ceiling; there's no way we could get to it here, but I have an idea. We can throw anything at it, see if the chandelier will move, and maybe knock down the TV remote.

We can even have a mattress or something soft at the bottom in case it does fall, so when it does fall, it won't break," he explained. Paulette was impressed with Sylvester's idea and ordered, "Yes, that's a good idea. Well done! Here's the plan: Sylvester and Theo will gather things to throw up at the chandelier and place them on the bed while I make a soft landing for the remote."

Sylvester and Theo ran downstairs and searched the whole house, trying to find as many things as they could fit in their hands to throw at the chandelier. They were still a bit scared, but they wanted to help Paulette. Meanwhile, Paulette took the mattress off the bed and placed it below the chandelier. She gathered cushions and anything soft she could find and put them around the mattress for more protection. She spent much time doing this because she wanted to get it done. She was sick of being in the cottage and wanted to find Kermit and Dora.

As she worked on her task, Paulette thought about Trevor and his second death. The memory of losing him broke her heart, and she knew it was something she would never get over. She will always remember him and hopes to see him again one day.

As they stood in the dimly lit basement, Paulette asked Sylvester if he had finished gathering things. Sylvester shook his head, indicating that he had yet to find everything on their list. Theo, who had been silently observing the exchange, came to Sylvester's defence, reminding Paulette that it was challenging to find and carry heavy items that were also safe to use.

Paulette nodded in understanding and then surprised them both by offering to help. Theo eagerly agreed, and the three of them searched for more items. Lost in their thoughts, they wondered how Trevor was doing and what he might be up to. Now and then, they would pause to examine an item, considering its usefulness and practicality.

Paulette interrupted their thoughts, asking if they had found anything yet. Theo apologised for being lost and told Paulette they had found more things. Paulette was pleased and suggested they try them out upstairs, eager to see how their new acquisitions would fare for the task.

Chapter 19

Teamwork

Paulette had an electrifying idea, "What if we spiced things up by taking turns throwing something at the chandelier? We can make a thrilling game out of it and have a blast. But we must ensure that we play fair, and nothing gets damaged." Theo quickly agreed, adding, "Let's make it more exciting by setting a target. Whoever hits the remote wins!" Paulette, being the fair leader, organised the order of turns, "Theo, you go first, followed by Sylvester, and then me." She also reminded them to be careful and not cause any harm.

The three of them put their items on the bed, which had no mattress. Theo picked up a towel and rolled it into a ball, securing it with an elastic band. He aimed the towel ball at the chandelier's light and threw it with all his might, but it only managed to wobble the light without hitting the remote. Next up was Sylvester, who picked up a fork and aimed at the chandelier. The fork made a few holes in the material, but the remote remained intact.

Paulette was up next, and she grabbed an empty water bottle. She took a deep breath and threw it with all her might. The bottle fell short of the chandelier and landed on the mattress. Feeling embarrassed, she apologised, but Theo and Sylvester cheered her on. Theo encouraged her, saying, "Don't give up, Paulette. You got this. Let's keep going and see who will hit the remote first!"

With the previous task completed, Theo, Paulette, and Sylvester were eager to move on to the next challenge. Theo proposed an ingenious idea and grabbed a bottle of washing-up liquid to use as a tool to retrieve the remote control. He aimed it perfectly, ensuring that the chandelier wouldn't get damaged, and threw it with just enough force to knock the remote onto the pillows without causing any harm. Paulette and Sylvester were amazed by Theo's quick thinking and praised him for his cleverness.

As they descended the stairs, they brainstormed the next step. Paulette suggested using the TV remote to turn on the TV, and everyone agreed that it was an excellent idea. Sylvester switched on the television, and to their surprise, Kermit appeared on the screen, revealing the next clue. The clue was clear, but they had to find the pond first. Sylvester remembered they had a map, but Paulette needed help remembering where it was. Fortunately, Sylvester knew where Trevor had left it, and Theo managed to locate it in

Trevor's backpack. According to the map, the pond was east of the cottage.

Paulette suggested that Sylvester put the potion bottle in a bag to prevent it from leaking. Theo was an expert with maps and volunteered to lead the way. They all agreed and set out on their adventure to find the pond.

The group of adventurers were making their way through the dense wilderness, daring to conquer any obstacle that stood in their way. Sylvester, always curious, politely probed Theo about how much longer it would take to reach their destination. Theo, the fearless leader, confidently responded that they were on the right track and would get their goal in no time. However, Paulette, who had been feeling uneasy from the start, voiced her concern about the possibility of camping outside without proper gear. But Theo, always the optimist, tried to calm her nerves by suggesting they complete their mission in record time. Paulette was partially convinced, but she trusted Theo's leadership.

As they marched on, Sylvester suddenly mentioned they were no longer the "After Life Crew" since their friend Trevor had parted ways with them. He suggested they develop a new name, but Paulette felt it was disrespectful to do so without Trevor. However, Theo, ever the voice of reason, encouraged them to move on and keep the original name. As they settled into their new surroundings, a rustling sound in the nearby bushes caught Paulette's attention. She was on high alert, but the others noticed nothing unusual. Despite their reassurances, Paulette remained uneasy as they continued their journey. But nothing could stop them from chasing their dreams and unravelling the secrets of the wilderness. The thrill of adventure grew stronger with each passing moment, and the team felt more alive.

As the After Life Crew ventured through the ominous forest, Paulette guarded the bag with the precious potion with her life, knowing that their entire mission hinged on it. As darkness descended and the rain pelted down upon them, Paulette's spirits dampened as she realised they were in for a long night. Theo apologised for his miscalculations, but his excuses wouldn't sway Paulette. Instead, she took charge and suggested they seek shelter from the storm. That's when Sylvester had a brilliant idea - they could call Kermit for help.

The group called out to Kermit, and within minutes, the rain began to ease up, and a small cottage materialised out of thin air. The After Life Crew couldn't believe their luck and eagerly ran inside to escape the storm. As they settled in for the night, they realised that they were in Kermit and Dora's cottage and that Kermit had moved it to a new location just for them. The cosy warmth of the cottage was a welcome relief from the harsh weather outside. The group breathed a sigh of relief as they relaxed, with Sylvester setting the precious potion on the table for all to see. Paulette and Theo shared the big, comfy bed while Sylvester made himself comfortable on the sofa. The group knew they still had a long journey ahead of them, but for now, they were safe, cosy, and grateful for Kermit's help.

Chapter 20

Transformation

As The After Life Crew members made their way towards the pond, they couldn't help but feel a little worn out and dreary from their journey. Despite their exhaustion, they knew they couldn't back out now, especially after Kermit's help. As Sylvester carried the precious potion in a bag, Theo pored over the map, and they continued walking east from their starting point. The journey felt endless, and Paulette couldn't help but express her frustration, "This trip could take days," she complained. Sylvester gently reminded her, "Yes, it could be a long journey, Paulette, but we have to finish it for Trevor, remember?" Paulette sighed and replied, "I know, but I'm so tired. I miss the old times when we would sit at home and not go out because we were too scared. The only one who used to go out was Trevor for food. I'm just worried about what we'll do without him. Who will cook our meals, and where will we get our food from?"

Theo chimed in, "I understand how you feel, Paulette. Living without your brother must be tough, but don't worry. We'll all pitch in. I'll go out and get the food, and we can all help with the cooking, cleaning, and shopping. Plus, we can all go out together to get the food if you want." Paulette was grateful for her friends' support. "Thank you, everyone. Even though Trevor's not here, I still have you both. You're great friends, and I'm glad you're with me. Promise me you won't leave me alone," she pleaded. "We promise," Theo and Sylvester replied in unison.

In the distance, the three adventurers finally caught sight of the vast pond, shimmering with a murky green hue that could only mean one thing - they were in hell. But they were undaunted as they gazed at the weeds growing along the edges, redolent with the smell of saltwater. A school of brilliant oranges and goldfish swam lazily around in the pond's depths while some tadpoles darted to and fro. On the other side, a small tree with a bird's nest beckoned, its branches reaching out in welcome. It was clear that they had arrived at the right place, and their hearts beat with excitement at the thought of what lay ahead.

The group of friends stood at the pond's edge, exhilarating and hopeful. Paulette had a brilliant idea to call out for Kermit and Dora to catch their attention, and the excitement was palpable. Theo was thrilled to reunite with his old pals after so many years, and the anticipation was almost too much to bear. Their first attempt was unsuccessful, and Paulette suggested they try calling out together, thinking that perhaps Theo's voice needed to be louder. With hearts pounding, they all shouted in unison, "Kermit, Dora!" after a brief moment of silence, they saw movement in the water. Suddenly, a slimy green frog leapt out of the pond and landed on a lily pad, followed by a beautiful bird that soared through the sky and perched on a nearby tree branch.

Kermit greeted them with uncontainable excitement, his voice echoing across the water. He explained that they had been waiting for someone to come for over twenty years and were over the moon to see Theo again. Dora spoke gently, expressing her condolences for hearing about Trevor's passing. Paulette explained that Trevor was their best friend and had recently passed away from a fall off a tree.

The group was devastated but knew they had to keep going for Trevor. Kermit was impressed that they had made the journey for Trevor, and they all shared a moment of silence for their lost friend. As they stood together, the air was electric, and the only sound was the gentle lapping of the water against the shore as they remembered Trevor.

“Wow! What an incredible journey we've been on! I've been there with you every step of the way, watching as you tackled every obstacle that came your way. And let me tell you, you crushed it! You rose to the occasion whenever you faced a challenge, showing incredible intelligence and teamwork. I was blown away by how you collaborated to decipher the map and find the pond.

And now, as a reward for all your hard work, I'm thrilled to offer you the chance to join me and Dora in our magical cottage! It may look small from the outside, but believe me, we can expand it to fit all of us with room to spare. We'll even create separate entrances for each of you. It's going to be amazing!

But before celebrating, we need to ensure you've completed the final task. Did you follow all the clues and use all the ingredients in the potion? And did you find a container to hold it? If so, congratulations! All that's left is to pour the potion into our mouths; we'll be eternally grateful. It's been an incredible journey, but we've made it. "Are you ready to complete our mission?" asked Kermit, with a glimmer of excitement in his eyes.

"We've been living in our makeshift homes for far too long. It's time to return to our human forms and live our lives fully." Sylvester was curious. "So, what have you both been up to all these years?" "Well," Dora chimed in, "I've been spending my days swimming in this pond while Kermit has been living in his bird's nest. But trust me, the real world is much nicer than our current abodes in hell." They all knew what had to be done. The potion was the only way to turn them back into humans. Sylvester took the bottle out of the bag as Kermit explained the process. "Who wants to go first?" Sylvester asked. Without hesitation, Kermit jumped in. "I do! I can't wait to have my legs again." The anticipation was palpable as Sylvester carefully poured the potion into Kermit's mouth, wondering what the future would hold for them once they were human again.

As the transformation of Kermit and Dora was completed, a sense of anticipation filled the air. Their animal bodies had metamorphosed into human forms, and it was clear that the After

Life Crew were surprised by what they saw. However, the tension between Kermit and Dora was palpable, and it seemed like their past was about to catch up with them. The After Life Crew thought their reunion might bring back old wounds, but they hoped for the best.

As Dora's frog body turned into a human one, she looked around with wonder and confusion. She had a human face with a mole on one side above her lip, but she was still a frog. Meanwhile, Kermit had transformed into an old, skinny man with a long white beard and small circular glasses. He wore a grey robe with multi-coloured stars and a pointed hat with the same pattern.

Dora was visibly angry at Kermit for turning her into a frog, and the Afte life Crew wondered if she would ever forgive him. However, while watching from the sidelines, Theo intervened and advised Dora to give Kermit another chance. He explained that Kermit had done what was best for the situation so that they could be together. Dora was hesitant at first, but she eventually agreed to forgive Kermit.

As Kermit apologised to Dora for his past mistakes, they both realised they had a new chance; the promise of a new life had filled the hearts of those who had been transformed. Dora, however, was still struggling to come to terms with the sudden change. She had yet to be consulted or informed beforehand, and the idea of giving up her human form so quickly was overwhelming. Despite her reservations, she was willing to forgive and move forward. Kermit, the group leader, reminded everyone of their promise to the heroes, and they all agreed to keep it.

Excitement filled the air as they discussed the prospect of finding a new home. Theo was enthusiastic about it, and Paulette seemed eager to explore their surroundings. However, a rustling sound in the bushes caused her to pause. It was not the first time she had heard it; it had been present on their previous journey to the pond. A sense of unease washed over her, and she couldn't shake off the feeling that they were being watched.

Dora proposed they return to the cottage, and Kermit wasted no time clapping his hands. Suddenly, the cottage appeared by the pond, leaving the After-Life Crew in awe. As they entered the cottage, they were amazed by the grandeur of their new home. Stairs led up to the second floor, with five bedrooms and a grand bathroom. Paulette, Theo, and Sylvester were thrilled to live there and couldn't wait to explore. However, before they could do so, a loud bang at the door interrupted their excitement.

Chapter 21

Giant Reptiles

As Dora and Kermit conversed, Dora inquired if they were expecting any guests. Kermit responded that it had been a long time since they had last received visitors. The After Life Crew, who were present, exchanged fearful glances as they had no idea who could be standing outside the front door. Paulette suggested they exercise caution and only open the door after first identifying the visitor. She recommended peering out of the window to get a glimpse of the person before opening the door. Kermit offered to take a look. He lifted the curtain and gazed out of the window. Surprisingly, he noticed a cluster of long-footed crocodiles waiting at the door with several others behind them. Paulette appeared puzzled and asked why there were crocodiles outside.

“A shrewd counsellor, Kermit, had alerted Dora and me about a potential danger. He had cautioned us that the crocodiles serving the powerful Serpent might have learned that we had been transformed back into humans. The Serpent was notorious for craving authority by any means possible, and he likely wanted to meet us. Theo, one of our companions, was understandably anxious about the crocodiles' probable aggression. However, Kermit had reassured us that they wouldn't dare harm anyone in Hell as it was against the Serpent's strict code of conduct.

With a deep breath, Kermit slowly opened the door, and we were astonished to find the crocodiles waiting for us. But instead of attacking, they lifted us and carried us on their backs, swimming through the dangerous waters towards the Serpent's castle. The journey was a mix of fear and bittersweet nostalgia as we passed by the familiar sights of Hell."

Finally, we arrived at the colossal castle, encircled by black gates and a moat of lava. The guards at the front gate interrogated us before allowing us entry, their eyes gleaming with suspicion. We couldn't help but wonder what fate awaited us within the walls of the Serpent's fortress.

Theo's heart raced as he approached the castle's gates, sensing the heat from within. He knew that trouble was brewing and his future was uncertain. All clad in black, the guards stood watchfully around the castle's perimeter. Despite their trepidation, Theo and Dora bravely walked past the crocodiles, who had been throwing off other travellers. Dora opened the gate with great hesitation, and they stepped inside. Before they could take another step, a vigilant guard emerged and stood in their path. The guard raised his voice and bellowed, "Halt! Who goes there?" The guard's eyes scanned them from head to toe as he fixed them with a stern and suspicious gaze, waiting for their response.

Kermit introduced himself, his wife Dora, and their three companions, Theo, Paulette, and Sylvester, to the guard. The guard warned them about the Serpent's intentions and let them through. As they crossed the bridge over the moat of lava, they were terrified because there were no railings, and the heat from the lava burned their faces. They tried to look straight ahead and ran to the other side once they were halfway through. Once they reached the castle, they heard growling and footsteps getting louder. They were greeted by a woman named Rita, who was dressed in a long black dress and had black hair that went past her shoulders. She politely introduced herself as Serpent's assistant and led them into the castle. Rita explained that she was forced to work for Serpent after she died, and she was still angry about it. She warned them that people who came to see Serpent usually did not come out. She revealed that she only confided in them because she knew they were friendly people who would do the right thing. She begged them not to tell Serpent anything about their conversation.

“We're so sorry, Rita. We won't tell Serpent a thing. Your secret is safe with us,” Dora reassured her.

“How do you know that we are nice people?” Paulette asked Rita.

As they followed Rita's lead, they arrived at a set of large doors adorned with the symbols of people's death. Rita confidently announced they had arrived and wished them good luck before opening the doors to reveal a small room. Inside, they saw two couches and a single chair, with Serpent sitting beside a fire pit that was the gateway to the souls. A small table was placed in the centre of the sofas, on which a candle and a statue of someone in misery were displayed. As soon as they entered, Rita closed the doors and stood by them, letting them walk towards Serpent. Serpent, who had already heard them coming, stood up and welcomed them with an evil grin.

The serpent's appearance was entirely unexpected. He had short, curly hair that reached the tips of his shoulders and a moustache but no beard. He wore a black shirt, baggy trousers, a jacket, and shoes. He wore a golden ring on his finger that matched a golden necklace. His overall appearance was quite striking and made a lasting impression on them.

Chapter 22

The Appearance of the Serpent

As they entered the room, Serpent gestured towards the two couches and said, "Come in, come in. Have a seat." They all complied and sat down nervously, wondering what Serpent wanted from them. As the bravest of the group, Kermit took the lead and asked, "What do you want from us?" Serpent replied, "I just wanted to talk to you." The way he said it was ominous, and everyone could sense that something was off.

Serpent continued, "I have to confess a couple of things, and I have some... news for you." His voice sounded evil, and the group exchanged worried glances. Sylvester, the most suspicious of them all, asked, "What news?"

The serpent paused before replying, "Do you think I don't know what you've been up to? I have been watching you since you stepped into the woods, just like Kermit was." This revelation surprised the group, and they wondered what other secrets the Serpent was hiding.

Sylvester spoke with an air of honesty, "We're sorry for our actions. We only went on an adventure because boredom had taken over us. We didn't intend to cause any harm." He continued, "You knew the Woods were forbidden, and yet you went there, Theo. You and Dora have lived in the forest your entire lives. Your parents even lost their lives there. If you were bored, you could have gone shopping, played a game, or risked your life again. But you disregard the rules and venture into the forbidden terrain."

Theo spoke tremblingly, "We apologise for our actions and didn't mean to upset you. We understand that we have caused an inconvenience and are sorry for that. Please don't hurt us. “I have been miserable all my life, so please don't make it worse. I beg of you."

Serpent sat down in his chair and looked sternly at Paulette. "I'd like to have a chat with you first. Let me see what you've been up to," he said. Paulette looked nervous as she sat across from him. Serpent's voice was cold and commanding as he continued, "Why did you go into the woods? Be honest!" Paulette took a deep breath before answering. "There were rumours that a witch and a wizard were still trapped in the woods," she began. "We wanted to help them and free them from their captivity."

Serpent's response was rude and dismissive. "Do you not think that if I wanted them to be human again, I would have done it myself by now?" His voice dripped with sarcasm. "Do you think I would have wanted someone else to do it? I didn't want them to be human. Kermit made a huge mistake, and now he has to pay the price."

The serpent's words took Paulette aback. She didn't know what Kermit had done or why he was being punished. Serpent's following words made her feel even worse. "It would have been better if you had just stayed in your demolished shelter, you homeless people," he sneered. Paulette felt a lump form in her throat as she struggled to hold back tears. "We are so sorry," she said in a small, innocent voice.

The group stood before the Serpent, hoping to receive guidance on their plan to free their friends Kermit and Dora. Theo explained that they had hoped to receive a reward for freeing the magical duo, possibly even a one-way ticket to heaven. However, the Serpent couldn't help but burst out laughing at their naivety. He explained that he gains power when anyone dies in hell, and as he is more potent than Kermit and Dora, there is no way they could send them to heaven. The group was disappointed to hear this, but Sylvester tried to find a silver lining by mentioning that they still received the reward of living with their friends in their cosy forest cottage.

The Serpent then changed the subject and asked about their friend Trevor. Paulette responded angrily as she explained that Trevor was dead and that the Serpent should have already known this since he seemed to be watching them closely.

"I forgot about that," Serpent sneered, a wicked glint in his eye. "I control everything that happens in hell - every time it rains, gets cold or turns dark, or when tree branches fall. It is all within my power." Paulette's jaw dropped in shock as she processed what she had just heard. She stood up from her seat and glared at Serpent, her voice shaking angrily. "You monster! You made the tree branch fall, and you made Trevor to die. Why would you do something so cruel?

"Serpent replied, "Where's the fun if you don't do something surprising? It was worth it. I prefer people to stay in their homes and only go out when they need to shop. As much as I love gaining power when someone dies, it wouldn't be fun if there wasn't anyone here. Then, I can't torture them, so I need to have some fun occasionally. People don't see me often, and when they do, I'll be too powerful for anybody."

Rita stood by the door, her heart racing with anticipation of the night ahead. Suddenly, a loud bang echoed through the room, causing her to jump in fright. Despite her fear, she composed herself and elegantly opened the door. To her disbelief, five enormous crocodiles with menacing teeth marched inside, their presence dominating the space. The guests all turned to face the unexpected guests, their expressions a mix of confusion and terror. The crocodiles advanced towards the chair belonging to the Serpent, their movements eerily silent and their intentions unknown. The tension in the room was palpable as everyone waited to see what would happen next.

"May I help you?" he asked while the crocodiles still waited and stared at him. "Here is your reward for fetching the fellow people," he said, remembering to hand over the reward. The serpent passed them a large plate full of the most gruesome thing ever; on the plate were human body parts that were ripped off from their limbs and torso. Paulette and Theo stood frozen, their eyes transfixed on the horrifying scene before them. With razor-sharp teeth, the crocodiles were devouring their meal with a bloodthirsty enthusiasm that made the young couple's stomachs turn. As soon as the reptiles finished eating, they nonchalantly slinked away, leaving behind a disgusted Rita, who promptly closed the door, hoping to forget the gruesome sight she had just witnessed.

As Sylvester and Paulette sat on the old, worn-out couch in Serpent's lair, they tried to make sense of the situation they had found themselves in. Serpent, their captor, had just made a snide remark about Paulette's brother, who had unfortunately fallen victim to Serpent's evil schemes. Feeling hurt and angry, Paulette defended her brother's honour and demanded that Serpent refrain from insulting him.

Trying to avoid the painful topic, Sylvester asked Serpent how the Crocodiles could track them down. Serpent revealed that he had already instructed the Crocodiles to follow their every move, explaining the rustling noises they had heard in the woods earlier. Paulette was shocked at the Serpent's cunning plan and impressed by his ability to manipulate their every move.

Serpent, enjoying the attention, mocked Paulette's brother's intelligence and praised Paulette for being much cleverer than him. This was the final straw for Paulette, who couldn't bear to hear any more insults about her beloved brother. She broke down in tears and admonished Serpent for his cruel words, reminding him of the terrible things he had done.

The atmosphere in the room was tense as Serpent, the self-proclaimed king of hell, exerted his dominance over the members of The After Life Crew. His voice was menacing as he warned them not to cross him or face dire consequences. Despite his threats, the group remained determined to stand up for themselves and their beliefs. As the conversation progressed, it became increasingly evident that Serpent had been watching the crew's every move. He even went as far as to use a magic candle to spy on them and learn about their activities. His constant surveillance had given him an edge, allowing him to uncover their secrets and plan his next move.

However, despite his power and control, only some were willing to bow down to Serpent's demands. Rita bravely spoke up and directly challenged him. She was tired of living under his rules and was ready to fight for her freedom and that of her companions.

As tensions continued escalating, Serpent rewarded the crew for their efforts by opening the gateway to the souls. But Paulette, another crew member, pleaded with him to reconsider, begging for one more chance to make things right. The crew was in for a challenging journey and an uncertain future.

"You should have considered the consequences before embarking on your foolish adventure. It's too late to turn back now," Serpent said with malice. "Please, Serpent, give them a chance. The adults can remain in the castle and work for you while you allow Theo and Paulette to leave. They're just children and are still uncertain about everything. Please don't follow through with this. You'll regret it," Rita pleaded with Serpent.

"I think having three more servants for the castle is a good idea, but I am unwilling to let the children go. Instead, they can also work for me as my servants. Here's my plan: Theo and Paulette will be my attendants, Kermit and Dora will assist me with the magic around here, and Sylvester can be my butler. I want to clarify that I am not planning to let you go anytime soon. You will work for me as long as I need you to," stated Serpent.

Rita suggested it was getting late and that the morning would be the best time to start working. She also thought that they might need to eat before retiring for the night. However, Serpent vehemently disagreed and forbade any food for the enslaved people, even using it as a pre-punishment tactic. Instead, he ordered Rita to show them to their quarters and ensure they stayed there until further notice. Rita promptly complied with his orders.

Chapter 23

Jiggery-Pokery

As Rita welcomed the five people into their small room, she couldn't help but feel a sense of anticipation. "Here is your room. Make yourself comfortable," she said, hoping the group would take her words to heart. Although the space was cramped, she hoped they would be okay with it.

Theo's uncertain response only fueled Rita's anticipation. She knew that the group was eager to leave this place, and she was ready to help them. "You don't have to lie. Tomorrow afternoon, I will secretly help you escape," she whispered, her heart beating faster with excitement.

Paulette's curiosity only added to Rita's anticipation. "Thank you, but why would you do that?" the woman asked. Rita's response was simple yet full of hope. "I know you are all good people, and I know Serpent will feed you to the souls even after you've worked here. But I want to avoid that. If I can't live my life, I should try to help you live yours. But keep this a secret, okay?"

Dora's gratitude and Theo's hunger were signs of what would come. Rita knew that the group was on her side and that they would do whatever it took to escape this place. "You're very kind, Rita. One day, we will rescue you," Dora said, her eyes filled with determination. "I wish that were possible," Rita sighed, knowing it was unlikely.

As Rita tiptoed out of the room, a glimmer of hope flickered in her heart, and she steeled herself to face whatever lay ahead. "I'm sorry, but I cannot bring you food. I don't want to alert Serpent to my actions. However, you will be provided food in the morning," she explained hushedly. Theo nodded in understanding, his stomach growling in protest. "I know; I feel bad about that. But we will figure something out," Rita reassured him with a kind smile.

"Who said we can't have food? Dora and I are magic. I can whip us up something to eat," Kermit suggested excitedly, earning a few surprised looks from the others. "That's a great idea, Kermit. But we must be careful not to alert Serpent," Rita responded, glancing around the room. "I understand," Kermit said with a nod. "Before we go to bed, I suggest we get some sleep. Serpent wakes up his staff early, like before dawn," Rita advised as she walked towards the door. "Goodnight, everyone!"

"How are we all going to fit on the bed?" Paulette complained, eyeing the small, rickety bed in the corner of the room. "We will all have to sleep on the bed. We'll figure it out later," Theo suggested, a hint of frustration in his voice.

The night was eerily silent, and the wind howled outside like a mournful cry. The five heard banging, screaming, and strange noises during the night, sending shivers down their spines. Kermit conjured up two more mattresses for himself and Dora, but he needed somewhere to sleep while the rest got the bed. They all managed to squeeze onto the bed, with Kermit and Sylvester sharing a mattress and one blanket.

Even though Theo had the bed, he still found it uncomfortable. The mattress was as hard as a rock, literally filled with stones. They were shocked about how much the Serpent wanted to torture them and his greediness. Luckily, Sylvester and Kermit got a comfortable, regular mattress that looked quite cosy. Theo regretted having the bed and should have gone on the mattress. Weirdly, Dora and Paulette were fast asleep on the rock-hard bed, and Theo thought it was because they were exhausted after everything they had been through.

As usual, Theo was awake, his mind racing about his life decisions. He knew, eventually, the Serpent would feed them to the souls. The haunting screams of the souls echoed in his mind, along with the raging anger of revenge, but he didn't know how to stop it. He could also hear Serpent screaming at Rita for making him look like a fool before and Rita shouting back, being brave. Theo thought about the broken hell and how unfair it was to everyone there. It was a pure tragedy, especially for him, and all he wanted was to be happy and live with his parents forever.

The night had been particularly restless for them, and they had barely managed to get any sleep. When Theo dozed off, the dawn had already broken, and he woke up to the sound of Paulette's voice yelling at him to get up. Rita sat beside him, stroking his head, and her beautiful face beamed with a smile as soon as Theo opened his eyes. She urged him to get up and get to work before Serpent woke up. Reluctantly, Theo got up, feeling immensely tired and wishing he could go back to sleep.

Paulette reminded everyone they had to wake up early lest they be fed to the souls. Dora spoke up, expressing her joy at finally being freed in the real world after waiting for over 20 years. However, she was saddened by the prospect of meeting the leader of hell, Serpent and being wholly eradicated. Rita intervened and convinced Serpent to spare their lives for a bit longer, allowing them to enjoy some precious moments together.

Theo felt dejected, knowing he would never be able to experience what it was like to be a werewolf like his parents. Paulette reminded him that they had to accept their fate and make the most of their time together. However, Dora had a brilliant idea that could change everything. While she and Kermit were in the potion room, they concocted a werewolf potion for Theo, allowing him to transform into a werewolf for two nights without needing a full moon. Theo was overjoyed and grateful, and Dora promised to keep it a secret with Rita's help.

Kermit thanked Theo for contributing to their escape plan and promised to reward him for his efforts. Although he had no rewards, he acknowledged everyone's hard work and thanked them, including Trevor, for their efforts.

Rita appeared at the door, and her voice cut through the silence. "Good morning, Theo!" she greeted, pushing open the scratched door. "You have five minutes to get ready, and then we must head to the Great Hall. I'll come collect you in five minutes and take you there." Paulette looked worried and asked a flurry of questions, "Is Serpent awake? Does he want to talk to us? Is he going to say he'll feed us to the souls?"

Rita tried calming her down and reassuring her that Serpent was still safe and asleep. She explained that they were going to the Great Hall to meet the others who worked at the castle. However, it wouldn't be an ordinary meet and greet, and the servants would only speak if spoken to by Serpent or Rita herself. If they were caught talking to the new guests, they would be punished severely and sometimes fed to the souls or sent to the dungeon.

Theo interrupted, "Wait! Before you go, we want to tell you something quickly." Rita went inside the room and closed the door, listening to them carefully. They confided in her that they planned to make a potion to turn Theo into a werewolf, and they needed her help to ensure that the Serpent didn't interfere. They feared it would spell bad news for them if he did.

Rita was excited at the prospect of helping Theo, and she shared her own experience with making potions and how it had helped a servant escape. She also revealed that she had a secret room in her quarters where Theo could transform into a werewolf without causing harm to anyone. Dora's face lit up with excitement at the prospect of having a safe place for Theo to transform. "That would be wonderful!" she said with a smile.

Chapter 24

Life of torment and Torture

As they followed Rita into the Great Hall, roaring souls echoed throughout the castle, filling everyone with fear. The doors of the Great Hall opened, and Rita welcomed them to the place. She introduced them to the various workers in the castle, from shafts to maidens to guards to servants, like herself. She also mentioned the people who worked for Serpent but didn't work in the castle, such as the boat drivers. The workers all wore the same uniform despite having different jobs. The girls wore a black dress, white tights, black shoes, a white smock, and the Harrow Pinner bun. The boys wore a black polo shirt, black trousers, black trainers, and a white pinafore.

Suddenly, a bell rang loudly, indicating it was time for the workers to start their duties. The five were initially slightly overwhelmed, but they quickly got to work. Kermit and Dora work on Theo's potion while Theo and Paulette clean Serpent's sitting room, where the souls are kept. Meanwhile, Sylvester started making Serpent's breakfast. Theo was exhausted from all the cleaning, but he knew this was the best thing ever happening to him.

As Paulette finished cleaning a section of the room, she asked Theo if he had finished cleaning the coffee table. Theo replied that he had and was putting the magical ornaments back on top. Paulette was pleased and said that they were almost done with the room. However, their work was interrupted by Serpent's angry voice, calling out to them from his bedroom.

Theo and Paulette rushed upstairs to find Serpent sitting on his bed, looking very angry.

The Serpent stood before the door; his face twisted in frustration as he rang the bell three times. As the two servants finally arrived, he yelled at them, "I rang this bell three times, and you still didn't come." One of the servants, Paulette, tried to defuse the situation by apologising and explaining that they were new and didn't know the significance of the bell's sound. However, Serpent was not pleased and scolded them for not being aware of the different bell sounds for other people. He reminded them they were his servants and should remember that for next time. The Serpent gave Paulette and Theo, the other servant, their morning duties. He instructed them to bring him a cup of hot human blood and a bowl of cereal when he rang the "servant bell" designated for his servants.

While the chefs would prepare the food, the servants were responsible for delivering it to him. Paulette couldn't help but express her disgust at the man's choice of drink, revealing her aversion to human blood. The serpent responded by telling his twisted nature, explaining that he enjoyed knowing the human he drank had suffered. He insisted that it was simply who he was.

As the two servants went to the kitchen to retrieve Serpent's breakfast, Paulette spoke with Sylvester, one of the chefs. She asked him how he was finding his work in the kitchen, to which he replied that it was "all right, but it could be better." He expressed shock at Serpent's eating and drinking habits, finding them extraordinary and gross.

Theo, another servant, chimed in, complaining about the serpent's rudeness and lack of consideration for those working in the house and the rest of the people in hell. Sylvester reminded them that the man was Serpent, the king of everyone's doom and that it was to be expected that he would treat people poorly. He explained that nobody in hell got paid and that the Serpent constantly gained more power. As he wandered, Paulette felt incredibly frustrated about how the Serpent treated them. She expressed her strong desire to take action against his unfair behaviour. However, Theo immediately cautioned her against doing anything that might endanger them. He reminded her they were lucky to have been saved from being fed to the souls by Rita.

Paulette couldn't help but agree with him. She had always been a bit of a risk-taker, but she knew that Theo was right. They were in a dangerous place and needed to be careful. She sighed deeply and said, "Perhaps you're right. Tragedy has followed me throughout my life, and unfortunately, it has continued into the afterlife.

I had hoped to go to heaven, make new friends, and live somewhere pleasant where I could be happy. Instead, I find myself stuck in this awful place. I was genuinely hoping for a better afterlife."

Theo nodded sympathetically. He knew exactly how she felt. They had both been through so much and being stuck in this place was challenging. But he knew that they had to keep their wits about them and stay safe. It was the only way they could survive in this strange, dangerous, and unpredictable world.

Sylvester spoke calmly to Paulette, "It's all right, Paulette. Everyone in hell wished they had gone to heaven, but unfortunately, it never happened. Life isn't always fair. At least in hell and Heaven, we can still act like we would in the real world, just slightly changed. But now, we are so close to feeling nothing, so we should try to make the most of it. We don't know when Serpent will turn us in, so we need to do everything to make him as happy as possible."

Theo agreed with Sylvester, "I agree with Sylvester. We can't always wish for some miracle. The only miracle we had was Rita, who is still willing to help us."

Suddenly, they heard the sound of a servant's bell ringing. "Quickly, you must go. Give this to Serpent and hurry up. We know he does not like to be kept waiting, and he is short-tempered. Make haste!" Sylvester directed.

Paulette and Theo quickly sprinted back to Serpent's bedroom, with Paulette carefully carrying his breakfast. Theo knocked on the door, looking scared. "Who is it." Serpent shouted. "It's... us," Theo stuttered. "Who's Us?" he yelled back. "Umm. It's Theo and Paulette with your breakfast," Theo replied nervously. "Come in! It's about time!" Serpent barked.

Both of them entered the room, which was dark and gloomy. "Did you get exactly what I wanted?" The serpent asked aggressively. "I think so, master," Paulette replied quickly. Serpent summoned them to come closer and peered down at the tray holding his food and drink. He snatched it speedily and ordered them to clean his library, but only his reading area and the bookshelf by the reading area. "You must finish it by the time I'm ready and come downstairs. Better hurry along because who knows when I'll get up?" he ordered them mysteriously.

Paulette and Theo quickly left the room and went to the kitchen to return the tray. Then, they headed to the library to begin cleaning.

Paulette and Theo were thrilled to be heading to the library. They had heard so much about it, and their expectations were high. When they finally arrived, they were left speechless by the place's grandeur. The towering wooden shelves, stacked with books of all shapes, sizes, and colours, were a sight to behold. The library was surprisingly vibrant, with walls painted dark, but the rest of the room was filled with life. The vast space was awe-inspiring, with ladders placed in different locations to reach the books stacked high on the shelves. The ceiling was breathtaking, painted black with silver stars twinkling randomly, a bright full moon hanging in one corner, and the planet Mars sitting in the other. As they looked around, they couldn't help but wonder if this library was magical. Was there a book hidden somewhere that could reveal the secret to getting to heaven? All these questions kept running through their minds.

Paulette couldn't contain her excitement, "Wow! This is amazing! Who knew Serpent likes to read? When he said 'library,' I thought he meant just one bookshelf with three or four books." Theo suggested they start cleaning and get the job done before Serpent returned. Without hesitation, they began sweeping the floor, dusting the bookshelves, polishing the bookshelf, rearranging the books, and putting them back neatly where they belonged. The job took longer than expected, and they were exhausted by the time they finished it, taking breaks in between.

Theo and Paulette had just finished cleaning the master's reading area when he walked in. They sat down on one of the couches to catch their breath, but their relaxation was short-lived as the master, Serpent, started yelling at them to get off his sofa. Trembling, they moved to the other side of the room and waited for him to say something.

Serpent inspected the reading area and found some dust on his bookshelf. He scolded them, saying they were the worst servants he'd ever had and threatened to feed them to his tortured family. Paulette apologised and offered to clean it again. Serpent accepted her apology but reminded them they only had ten minutes for their break.

As they left the library, Paulette bravely asked Serpent about the leader of the afterlife and his rules. Serpent explained that he had to obey the leader's rules, and the more power he gained, the more he could take over by becoming the leader himself. He also told them they could only go to the kitchen, potion room, or bedroom during their ten-minute break, leaving them curious about what other secrets this mysterious place held. Feeling relieved they wouldn't be fed to Serpent's tortured family, Theo and Paulette left the room searching for Sylvester, wondering what other secrets the afterlife held.

Chapter 25

Serpent's Fury

After a long and arduous workday, Paulette, Sylvester, and Theo were utterly exhausted. They were drained and in dire need of a break. Paulette suggested they visit the potion room to see Kermit and Dora and recharge their energies. When they arrived, they found Kermit and Dora working on a top-secret potion, which they had to keep hidden from everyone else. Only Rita was aware of their plans. As the day turned into night, the excitement among the workers grew as they finished their tasks. Rita led everyone to her secret room, which was pitch black except for a faint light from a wall lamp. Theo eagerly anticipated drinking the potion, but before he could, there was a knock at the door, and heavy footsteps approached.

Suddenly, the Serpent appeared, yelling at everyone to follow him. Theo dropped the potion, spilling it on the ground as they all rushed to follow Serpent to his sitting area where the souls' cage was kept. The workers sat down nervously, wondering what Serpent was going to do. Serpent demanded to know what they were doing, but Sylvester lied, saying they were playing a game in the dark. However, the Serpent saw through the lie and accused them of trying to escape by asking for a potion. Theo spoke up and told Serpent the truth about the potion, explaining that Kermit and Dora were making it so he could turn into a werewolf-like his parents for a few days. Serpent demanded to know why, but tension hung in the air before Theo could answer.

“Because I never got to live my life fully, and the potion my parents gave me will wear off when I am eighteen. I don’t think I will be in hell until eighteen, so I wanted to experience being a werewolf before I went.” “Did I tell you that you could do this? Did you hear me say I gave my permission? I don’t think so. You live with me now, and you obey me. Never do things behind my back ever again.” Serpent sarcastically said. Theo sat back down in disappointment.

“Rita, I am disappointed and hurt by your recent actions. Your decision to share secret information with others without my consent has violated our understanding and compromised my authority. As a result, I have been left feeling distressed and angry towards you and everyone else involved. Your actions have betrayed my trust and have caused irrevocable damage to our relationship. I need to hold you accountable for your behaviour, and I expect everyone complicit in the breach to face the consequences of their actions. I hope this serves as a lesson to all involved that such acts of betrayal will not be tolerated.

Rita's heart raced as she pleaded with Serpent, the feared leader of hell. She knew she had broken the rules by helping someone but couldn't bear to see them suffer. "Please, Serpent," she begged, "punish me if you must but spare them. I was wrong, but it was the least I could do. They've done so much for me; I couldn't just stand by and watch them suffer. Can't you show some sympathy for once?"

Serpent's eyes narrowed as he looked down at Rita. "Being mean is what I live for," he hissed. "Hell isn't about happiness. It's pure sorrow. You, of all people, should know this. Because you deliberately disobeyed me, you will certainly get punished now." With a flick of his wrist, he produced a minor silver key and strode towards the sturdy gates that led to the cage of souls.

Rita trembled as Serpent unlocked the gate, and the roars of the damned filled the room. The colours of black, orange, and yellow swirled around them, and the shapes of angry people could be seen inside the cage. Smoke and scorching fire poured out of the opening, filling the room with a suffocating heat. Everyone in the room, except for Serpent, was terrified, feeling like they had been plunged into the molten moat surrounding his castle.

The atmosphere was tense as Serpent, the sinister taskmaster, stood before a group of trembling souls. "Who’s going to go in first?" he asked, his voice dripping with malice. "Or should we do it in pairs?" The air fell silent, punctuated only by the anguished cries of previous victims.

"Is nobody going to talk?" Serpent sneered. "Then I guess I will have to do it for you. Kermit and Dora can go first, then. Off you go!" With shaking legs, the pair stepped forward, their fear palpable. "It's been nice knowing you guys. Goodbye!" Kermit said, clinging tightly to Dora's hand. With a wave, they were pushed into the flames, their screams ringing out before being abruptly silenced.

The remaining group members - Theo, Paulette, Sylvester and Rita - shrank in terror. "Who's next?" Serpent demanded. "How about Theo and Paulette go?" With a forceful shove, the pair stumbled forward, desperately trying to resist.

"Come on, Paulette," Theo whispered urgently. "What's the point of living in hell if we have to work all day for Serpent? It's boring. It might be better just not doing anything." Paulette trembled, her fear almost overwhelming, but

Theo's words gave her courage. "I get what you're saying, but I'm scared," she replied.

"It's OK to be scared, but I'll be with you so that you won't do it alone," Theo said, his voice steady. "Have fun perishing together, especially you, Theo," Serpent jeered. "After everything, even in the real world and when you did your tasks, it was all for nothing." Before Serpent could push them, they jumped in, their cries of terror mixing with those of Kermit and Dora.

Serpent, a mysterious and foreboding figure with a twisted smile, stood at the centre of the cage, his eyes gleaming with evil energy. Despite Sylvester's brave exterior, he couldn't help but feel a sense of dread as he stepped into the cage, knowing the danger that awaited him. Serpent was known for his love of the screams, roars, and cries of agony that echoed through the arena, and Sylvester knew that he was no match for the evil entity.

As the crowd watched in horror, Serpent's attention quickly shifted to Rita, who sat at the edge of the cage, her eyes wide with fear. The serpent began chatting with her amicably, relishing in the misery and horror of those under his control. The atmosphere was tense, and the onlookers could feel the fear and uncertainty radiating from Sylvester and the others.

With his heart pounding in his chest, Sylvester stood alone in the centre of the arena, surrounded by walls of flames that sent waves of heat rippling across his skin. Despite the fear that threatened to overwhelm him, he stood tall, his eyes fixed on the massive serpent that slithered towards him, its malevolent gaze fixed on its prey. The screams and roars of the other captives echoed in his ears, a constant reminder of the fate that awaited him. But Sylvester refused to break under the pressure, his resolve unwavering as he took a deep breath and jumped into the fray, ready to face whatever lay ahead.

As Rita stood before the Serpent, her body trembled with fear and desperation. She could feel his cold and unfeeling gaze upon her. His voice was like ice as he asked her the question that sank her heart. "Are you ready?" she knew what was coming next, and the mere thought made her feel sick. She tried to plead with him, "No! Please don't do this to me. I'll do anything to make it right. I'll be your most loyal assistant!" But her words fell on deaf ears as Serpent stared at her, his expression unreadable.

Reluctantly, Rita trailed behind Serpent, her eyes fixed on his every move as he led her towards a foreboding structure. As they approached the entrance for souls, Rita leaned in to take a closer look. Suddenly, without warning, Serpent gave her a forceful shove, sending her tumbling into the fiery depths of the enclosure. The flames roared around her, engulfing her in a blaze of torment and agony.

Serpent cackled as he slithered away from the enclosure, locking the gates behind him. He made his way back to his lair, a contented smile on his face as he propped up his feet in satisfaction. The souls he had imprisoned would never be free again, and he revelled in the power he held over them. With a sinister tone, he spoke to the souls, "Enjoy the people." His words hung in the air, reminding those who crossed him of the dark fate that awaited him. The souls were trapped in the enclosure, doomed to suffer for eternity, and the Serpent was pleased with the outcome.

Chapter 26

The Point of No Return

The After Life Crew had been a group of young and fearless individuals who had devoted their entire lives to unravelling the mysteries of what lies beyond death. They had embarked on a dangerous quest that had led them to the very edge of existence, where they had made a remarkable discovery that shook the foundations of their beliefs. They had found not one but two afterlives that awaited us after we passed away. The first afterlife they had discovered was the realm of hell, where the wicked souls were punished and tormented for their sins. It was a place of endless agony and suffering, where the damned were subjected to eternal damnation and despair.

The second afterlife was the realm of nothingness, where the soul existed, devoid of any sensation, feeling, or purpose. It was a place of emptiness and oblivion, where the soul drifted aimlessly without any sense of direction or meaning. When the news of the After Life Crew's fate reached Theo's parents, Zoe and Eugene, they were devastated. Their beloved son had been a crew member, and they had always known that his search for knowledge would take him to dangerous territories. However, they had never anticipated that he would end up in the second afterlife, where they could never hope to see him again. The news hit them like a ton of bricks, and they broke down in inconsolable tears. They had already lost their child to hell, and now this.

Despite their overwhelming grief, Zoe and Eugene still felt a faint whisper of Theo's voice in their hearts, like a distant echo trying to reach them from beyond the veil of death. At first, they thought it was just their imagination, a desperate attempt to cling to the memory of their son. But the more they listened, the more convinced they became that it was real. They shared their experiences with others but were met with scepticism and disbelief. It wasn't until they approached the leader of heaven that they found someone willing to listen to their story. To their amazement, the leader confirmed that a select few parents had experienced this phenomenon, where they could hear their child's voice even in the afterlife. It was a rare occurrence, but it was real.

This revelation gave Zoe and Eugene hope and comfort, knowing their bond with Theo was still alive. They clung to his voice, hoping it would help them navigate the dark times ahead. They knew that they might never see him again, but they refused to let go of the hope that someday they would be reunited with their son in a happier place, where there would be no more pain, no more suffering, and no more goodbyes.

Author's Biography

William is a talented author who has written several captivating books, including 'Forbidden Terrain,' 'Unmarksked: History of Alkebula,' and 'Betwixt 2 Shores.' The latter, launched in September 2023, was attended by many renowned guests, such as Her Excellency Dr Karen May Hill OBE and Gary Heather, Mayor of Islington Council.

William is a noteworthy figure in Antigua, as he is the first non-fictional male writer to have gained international recognition. He holds a Master's in Adult Education from Goldsmiths College, University of London. He has a wealth of experience in teaching, having spent eighteen years teaching English Language at one of the top FE Colleges in London. During his tenure, the college was awarded twice for Excellence in Education by the late Queen Elizabeth 2nd, and William was fortunate enough to be employed during both awards ceremonies.

Printed in Great Britain
by Amazon

45381252R00175